Doris Lessing

was born of British parents in Persia (now Iran) in 1919 and was taken to Southern Rhodesia (now Zimbabwe) when she was five. She spent her childhood on a large farm there and first came to England in 1949. She brought with her the manuscript of her first novel, *The Grass is Singing*, which was published in 1950 with outstanding success in Britain, in America, and in ten European countries. Since then her international reputation not only as a novelist but as a non-fiction and short-story writer has flourished. For her collection of short novels, *Five*, she was honoured with the 1954 Somerset Maugham Award. She was awarded the Austrian State Prize for European Literature in 1981, and the German Federal Republic Shakespeare Prize of 1982. Among her other celebrated novels are *The Golden Notebook*, *The Summer Before the Dark*, *Memoirs of a Survivor* and the five-volume *Children of Violence* series. Her short stories have been collected in a number of volumes including *To Room Nineteen* and *The Temptation of Jack Orkney*; while her African stories appear in *This Was the Old Chief's Country* and *The Sun Between Their Feet*. *Shikasta*, the first in a series of five novels with the overall title of *Canopus in Argos: Archives*, was published in 1979. Her novel *The Good Terrorist* won the W. H. Smith Literary Award for 1985, and the Mondello Prize in Italy that year. *The Fifth Child* won the Grinzane Cavour Prize in Italy, an award voted on by students in their final year at school. *The Making of the Representative for Planet 8* was made into an opera with Philip Glass, libretto by the author, and premièred in Houston. Her most recent works include *London Observed* and *African Laughter*.

Novels

The Grass is Singing
The Golden Notebook
Briefing for a Descent into Hell
The Summer Before the Dark
Memoirs of a Survivor
Diary of a Good Neighbour
If the Old Could . . .
The Good Terrorist
The Fifth Child

'Canopus in Argos: Archives'
series

Re: Colonised Planet 5,
Shikasta
The Marriages Between Zones
Three, Four, and Five
The Sirian Experiments
The Making of the
Representative for Planet 8
Documents Relating to the
Sentimental Agents in the
Volyen Empire

'Children of Violence'
novel sequence

Martha Quest
A Proper Marriage
A Ripple from the Storm
Landlocked
The Four-Gated City

Drama

Play with a Tiger
Each His Own
The Singing Door

Short Stories

Five
The Habit of Loving
A Man and Two Women
The Story of a Non-Marrying
Man and Other Stories
Winter in July
The Black Madonna
This Was the Old Chief's
Country (Collected African
Stories, Vol. 1)
The Sun Between Their Feet
(Collected African Stories,
Vol. 2)
To Room Nineteen (Collected
Stories, Vol. 1)
The Temptation of Jack Orkney
(Collected Stories, Vol. 2)
London Observed

Poetry

Fourteen Poems

Non-fiction

In Pursuit of the English
Particularly Cats
Rufus the Survivor
Going Home
A Small Personal Voice
Prisons We Choose to Live
Inside
The Wind Blows Away Our
Words
African Laughter

DORIS LESSING

A Small Personal Voice

Essays, Reviews, Interviews

Edited and introduced by Paul Schlueter

Flamingo
An Imprint of HarperCollinsPublishers

Flamingo
An Imprint of HarperCollins*Publishers*
77–85 Fulham Palace Road,
Hammersmith, London W6 8JB

First published in Great Britain by Flamingo 1994
9 8 7 6 5 4 3 2 1

First published by Alfred A. Knopf, Inc., US in 1974
Copyright © Doris Lessing 1956, 1957, 1959, 1963, 1966, 1968,
1971, 1972, 1974

'Interview with Doris Lessing' by Roy Newquist, from
Counterpoint by Roy Newquist, copyright © Rand McNally 1964.
'Doris Lessing at Stony Brook', copyright © Jonah Raskin 1970.
'Vonnegut's Responsibility', copyright © The New York Times
Company 1973. Reprinted by permission.

'Impertinent Daughters' first published by *Granta* in two parts.
'Doris Lessing: Impertinent Daughters' copyright © Doris Lessing
1984, 1985, and 'Doris Lessing: My Mother's Life (Part Two)',
copyright © Doris Lessing 1985, 1986.

The Author asserts the moral right to
be identified as the author of this work

Photograph of Doris Lessing © Ingrid von Kruse

ISBN 0 00 654759 1

Set in Linotron Sabon

Printed in Great Britain by
HarperCollinsManufacturing Glasgow

CONTENTS

INTRODUCTION
BY PAUL SCHLUETER

Although most readers of Doris Lessing know her only through her novels and stories, she has also written many essays and given a number of interviews that shed considerable light on her ideas about and commitment to the craft of writing. Increasingly, scholars and others have asked for copies of specific pieces no longer in print or otherwise unavailable, and it is for this reason that this selection has been prepared.

A few words about the selections seem appropriate. The initial piece, 'The Small Personal Voice,' appeared in *Declaration* (London: MacGibbon and Kee, 1957, pp. 11-27) and is Mrs Lessing's most affirmative essay concerned with the function of the novel in an age of cataclysmic change. Other writers included in *Declaration* were John Osborne, Colin Wilson, John Wain, and Kenneth Tynan.

The Preface to *The Golden Notebook*, Mrs Lessing's most famous and justly praised novel, was written in 1971 for a paperback reprint of the book first published a decade earlier, and appears in both the current British and American editions of the book (London: Michael Joseph and Panther Books, New York: Simon & Schuster and Bantam Books). It also appeared, as 'On *The Golden Notebook*', in *Partisan Review*, XL, 1 (1973), pp. 14–30. It is Mrs Lessing's fullest statement thus far about the novel and is a healthy corrective to numerous misunderstandings and misinterpretations made previously by reviewers and critics.

The interview conducted by Roy Newquist took place in

October 1963 and was published in Newquist's book *Counterpoint* (Chicago: Rand McNally,1964, pp. 413–24). Jonah Raskin's interview, 'Doris Lessing at Stony Brook: An Interview,' was conducted in May 1969 during a time when Mrs Lessing was spending four days at the State University of New York at Stony Brook and was published in *New American Review 8* (New York: New American Library, 1970, pp. 166-79); at the time the Stony Brook campus was undergoing the agonies of political struggle between the activists among the students and the outside authorities, and the interview is more than anything else a dialogue between the two generations of political radicals. Florence Howe's interview 'A Talk with Doris Lessing,' was conducted in October 1966 and published in *The Nation*, March 6, 1967, pp. 311–13.

Concluding the first section of the book is a piece in which Mrs Lessing discusses her childhood. 'My Father' first appeared in the *Sunday Telegraph* on September 1, 1963, and later appeared in *Vogue*, in an abridged form, as 'All Seething Underneath' (February 15, 1964, pp. 80–1, 132–3).

The second section of this book includes a number of Mrs Lessing's essays about and reviews of the work of other writers. Readers of her 'Children of Violence' series will recognize her frequent references to Olive Schreiner's *The Story of an African Farm* (1883) as suggestive of a debt owed by one writer to another, so Mrs Lessing's 'Afterword' to a recent reprint of the novel (New York: Fawcett World Library, 1968, pp. 273–90) is especially timely. 'Allah Be Praised' is a review of *The Autobiography of Malcolm X*, and appeared in the *New Statesman* (May 27, 1966, pp. 775, 778).

'In the World, Not of It' is one of two essays Mrs Lessing has written about the writings of Idries Shah, and appeared in *Encounter* (August, 1972, pp. 61–4). Another piece, 'An

Ancient Way to New Freedom,' originally appeared in *Vogue* for September 15, 1971, and is not included in the present selection because of its availability in a collection entitled *The Diffusion of Sufi Ideas in the West*, edited by L. Lewin (Boulder, Colo.: Keysign Press, 1972).

'Vonnegut's Responsibility' suggests Mrs Lessing's interest in writers of our own day, an interest found in her occasional reviews of current books. The essay appeared in the *New York Times Book Review* (February 4, 1973, p. 35). Eugène Marais's *The Soul of the White Ant* was first published in 1937 (translated from Afrikaans) and reissued in 1969; Mrs Lessing's essay – really more of a tribute than a mere commentary – appeared in the *New Statesman*, January 29, 1971 under the title 'Ant's Eye View.'

And, finally, 'A Deep Darkness' is a review of Isak Dinesen's (pseudonym of Karen Blixen) *Shadows on the Grass* (1961), but with as much to offer on Blixen's *Out of Africa* (1938) as on the more recent book; since both concern the Danish author's love for and years of residence in Africa, it seems appropriate that Doris Lessing offer such a review. The piece appeared in the *New Statesman*, January 15, 1971, pp. 87–8.

The book ends with a short group of selections about Africa, the subject of many earlier pieces by Mrs Lessing. 'Being Prohibited' describes her visit to South Africa in 1956, following which she was placed on the list of 'prohibited aliens' for that country and Southern Rhodesia. The essay was first published in the *New Statesman* (April 21, 1956, pp. 410, 412), and should be read in conjunction with Mrs Lessing's book *Going Home* (1957) in which she provides a detailed account of what she found in colonial Africa.

'The Fruits of Humbug' appeared in *The Twentieth Century* (April 1959, pp. 368–76) as part of a series entitled 'Crisis in Central Africa,' and compares Mrs Lessing's own return to Africa in 1956 with the expulsion of a Member of Parliament from Rhodesia in 1959.

Mrs Lessing's range of subjects is wide, and her interest in the essay continues year after year. This selection ought to serve well to introduce a different facet of her talent to a popular audience, and to provide the difficult-to-locate materials scholars around the world have been requesting. And the several interviews included enable Mrs Lessing to offer more detailed remarks about her own craft of writing than are otherwise available to a popular audience, and provide even greater understanding of this most gifted writer to the many who enjoy her fiction.

On Her Life
and Writings

The Small Personal Voice

To say, in 1957, that one believes artists should be committed, is to arouse hostility and distrust because of the quantities of bad novels, pictures, and films produced under the banner of committedness; also because of a current mood of reaction against socialist art-jargon, the words and phrases of which have been debased by a parrot-use by the second-rate to a point where many of us suffer from a nervous reluctance to use them at all. The reaction is so powerful and so prompt that one has only to stand up on a public platform and say that one still believes in the class analysis of society and therefore of art, in short that one is a marxist, for nine-tenths of the audience immediately to assume that one believes novels should be simple tracts about factories or strikes or economic injustice.

I see no reason why good writers should not, if they have a bent that way, write angry protest novels about economic injustice. Many good writers have. Dickens, for instance, was often inspired by poverty and injustice. Novels like *Germinal* or *The Jungle* are not to be despised. A writer's natural talent may drive him to transform what might have been a simple morality tale into something much more powerful. Or his talent may be adequate only for crude protest. But propagandist literature, religious or political, is as old as literature itself, and has sometimes been good and sometimes bad.

7

Recently it has been very bad; and that is why the idea of committedness is in disrepute. But at least it is in debate, and that is a good thing: passionate polemics about art or about anything else are always a sign of health.

Polemics about art now must take into account what has happened in the communist countries where socialist theories of art have been put into practice. The 'agonized reappraisals' that are going on everywhere in the socialist movements are a seminal force; for I do not believe that humanity is so compartmented that reappraisals, agonized or not, can go on in one section of it and not quickly and usefully influence anybody who thinks at all.

As a writer I am concerned first of all with novels and stories, though I believe that the arts continuously influence each other, and that what is true of one art in any given epoch is likely to be true of the others. I am concerned that the novel and the story should not decline as art-forms any further than they have from the high peak of literature; that they should possibly regain their greatness. For me the highest point of literature was the novel of the nineteenth century, the work of Tolstoy, Stendhal, Dostoevsky, Balzac, Turgenev, Chekhov; the work of the great realists. I define realism as art which springs so vigorously and naturally from a strongly held, though not necessarily intellectually defined, view of life that it absorbs symbolism. I hold the view that the realist novel, the realist story, is the highest form of prose writing; higher than and out of the reach of any comparison with expressionism, impressionism, symbolism, naturalism, or any other ism.

The great men of the nineteenth century had neither religion nor politics nor aesthetic principles in common. But what they did have in common was a climate of ethical judgement; they shared certain values; they were humanists. A nineteenth-century novel is recognizably a nineteenth-century novel because of this moral climate.

If there is one thing which distinguishes our literature, it is a confusion of standards and the uncertainty of values. It would be hard, now, for a writer to use Balzacian phrases like 'sublime virtue' or 'monster of wickedness' without self-consciousness. Words, it seems, can no longer be used simply and naturally. All the great words like love, hate; life, death; loyalty, treachery; contain their opposite meanings and half a dozen shades of dubious implication. Words have become so inadequate to express the richness of our experience that the simplest sentence overheard on a bus reverberates like words shouted against a cliff. One certainty we all accept is the condition of being uncertain and insecure. It is hard to make moral judgements, to use words like good and bad.

Yet I reread Tolstoy, Stendhal, Balzac, and the rest of the old giants continuously. So do most of the people I know, people who are left and right, committed and uncommitted, religious and unreligious, but who have at least this in common, that they read novels as I think they should be read, for illumination, in order to enlarge one's perception of life.

Why? Because we are in search of certainties? Because we want a return to a comparatively uncomplicated world? Because it gives us a sense of safety to hear Balzac's thundering verdicts of guilt or innocence, and to explore with Dostoevsky, for instance in *Crime and Punishment*, the possibilities of moral anarchy, only to find order restored at the end with the simplest statements of faith in forgiveness, expiation, redemption?

Recently I finished reading an American novel which pleased me; it was witty, intelligent, un-self-pitying, courageous. Yet when I put it down I knew I would not reread it. I asked myself why not, what demand I was making on the author that he did not answer. Why was I left dissatisfied with nearly all the contemporary novels I read? Why, if I were reading for my own needs, rather than for the

9

purposes of informing myself about what was going on, would I begin rereading *War and Peace* or *The Red and the Black*?

Put directly, like this, the answer seemed to me clear. I was not looking for a firm reaffirmation of old ethical values, many of which I don't accept; I was not in search of the pleasures of familiarity. I was looking for the warmth, the compassion, the humanity, the love of people which illuminates the literature of the nineteenth century and which makes all these old novels a statement of faith in man himself.

These are qualities which I believe are lacking from literature now.

This is what I mean when I say that literature should be committed. It is these qualities which I demand, and which I believe spring from being committed; for one cannot be committed without belief.

Committed to what? Not to being a propagandist for any political party. I never have thought so. I see no reason why writers should not work, in their role as citizens, for a political party; but they should never allow themselves to feel obliged to publicize any party policy or 'line' unless their own private passionate need as writers makes them do so: in which case the passion might, if they have talent enough, make literature of the propaganda.

Once a writer has a feeling of responsibility, as a human being, for the other human beings he influences, it seems to me he must become a humanist, and must feel himself as an instrument of change for good or for bad. That image of the pretty singer in the ivory tower has always seemed to me a dishonest one. Logically he should be content to sing to his image in the mirror. The act of getting a story or a novel published is an act of communication, an attempt to impose one's personality and beliefs on other people. If a writer accepts this responsibility, he must see himself, to use the socialist phrase, as an architect of the soul, and it is a phrase which none of the old nineteenth-century novelists would have shied away from.

But if one is going to be an architect, one must have a vision to build towards, and that vision must spring from the nature of the world we live in.

We are living at a time which is so dangerous, violent, explosive, and precarious that it is in question whether soon there will be people left alive to write books and to read them. It is a question of life and death for all of us; and we are haunted, all of us, by the threat that even if some madman does not destroy us all, our children may be born deformed or mad. We are living at one of the great turning points of history. In the last two decades man has made an advance as revolutionary as when he first got off his belly and stood upright. Yesterday, we split the atom. We assaulted that colossal citadel of power, the tiny unit of the substance of the universe. And because of this, the great dream and the great nightmare of centuries of human thought have taken flesh and walk beside us all, day and night. Artists are the traditional interpreters of dreams and nightmares, and this is no time to turn our backs on our chosen responsibilities, which is what we should be doing if we refused to share in the deep anxieties, terrors, and hopes of human beings everywhere.

What is the choice before us? It is not merely a question of preventing an evil, but of strengthening a vision of a good which may defeat the evil.

Even before we liberated the power in the atom, so socialist economists claim, the products of our labour (that is, if freed from the artificial restrictions of a strangling economic system) were enough to feed and clothe all the people in the world; humanity could have been freed from want and drudgery if we had taken the brakes off the machines and if so much of the wealth we produced had not been spent on the engines of war. Even before we split the atom, the old dream of man liberated from the tyrannies of hunger and of cold had the solidity of something possible.

But to imagine free man, leisured man, is to step outside what we are. There is no one on this earth who is not twisted by fear and insecurity, and the compromise of thinking made inevitable by want and fear. Those people who see leisured man in terms of football matches and television-watching; those who say: 'You can't give man leisure, he won't know how to use it,' are as much victims of a temporary phase of economic development as the coupon-fillers and the screen-dreamers. Their imaginations are in bond to their own necessities. Slaves can envy the free; slaves can fight to free their children; but slaves suddenly set free are marked by the habits of submission; and slaves imagining freedom see it through the eyes of slaves.

I am convinced that we all stand at an open door, and that there is a new man about to be born, who has never been twisted by drudgery; a man whose pride as a man will not be measured by his capacity to shoulder work and responsibilities which he detests, which bore him, which are too small for what he could be; a man whose strength will not be gauged by the values of the mystique of suffering.

The imagination of the world already rejects hunger and poverty. We all believe they can be abolished. If humanity submits to living below the level of what is possible, it will be as shameful as when a human being chooses to live below the level of what he can be; or a nation falls below itself.

There are only two choices: that we force ourselves into the effort of imagination necessary to become what we are capable of being; or that we submit to being ruled by the office boys of big business, or the socialist bureaucrats who have forgotten that socialism means a desire for goodness and compassion – and the end of submission is that we shall blow ourselves up.

It is because it is so hard to think ourselves into the possibilities of the ancient dream of free man that the nightmare is so strong. Everyone in the world now has moments when he throws down a newspaper, turns off the radio, shuts his ears to the man on the platform, and holds out his hand and looks at it, shaken with terror. The hand of a white man, held to the warmth of a northern indoor fire; the hand of a black man, held into the strong heat of the sun: we look at our working hands, brown and white, and then at the flat surface of a wall, the cold material of a city pavement, at breathing soil, trees, flowers, growing corn. We think: the tiny units of the matter of my hand, my flesh, are shared with walls, tables, pavements, trees, flowers, soil . . . and suddenly, and at any moment, a madman may throw a switch, and flesh and soil and leaves may begin to dance together in a flame of destruction. We are all of us made kin with each other and with everything in the world because of the kinship of possible destruction. And the history of the last fifty years does not help us to disbelieve in the possibility of a madman in a position of power. We are haunted by the image of an idiot hand, pressing down a great black lever; or a thumb pressing a button, as the dance of fiery death begins in one country and spreads over the earth; and above the hand the concentrated fanatic stare of a mad sick face.

Even the vision of the madman it not so bad. We are all of us, at times, this madman. Most of us have said, at some time or another, exhausted with the pressure of living 'Oh for God's sake, press the button, turn down the switch, we've all had enough.' Because we can understand the madman, since he is part of us, we can deal with him, he is not so frightening as that other image: of a young empty-faced technician in

13

anonymous overalls, saying 'Yes sir!' and pressing the button. The anonymous technician, one of the growing army manning the departments of death, has no responsibility. He might turn the switch looking over his shoulder for confirmation at the Chairman of the Committee who ordered him to do it. And the Committee to another Committee. And the Chairman of that final superior Committee, one of those little half-men that we see on the newsreels, with their self-consciously democratic faces – that Chairman will say: 'I represent the people.' And the people is the brown man sitting under a tree, holding out the flesh of his forearm to the heat of the sun, thinking that the warmth of the great sun is the warmth also of that final blast of heat; the people is me.

Now, in March 1957, the British Government decides to continue the hydrogen bomb tests which threaten unborn children. Yet of the men who took the decision I am sure there is not one who says: Because of me thousands of children will be born crippled, blind, deaf, mad. They are members of a committee. They have no responsibility as individuals. They represent me. But I repudiate their act. I don't know one person, have never known a person, who would agree, as an individual, to throw that particular switch which will make children be born monsters. We all know there is a terrible gap between the public and the private conscience, and that until we bridge it we will never be safe from the murderous madman or the anonymous technician. But what is the nature of that gap? Partly, I think, it is that we have been so preoccupied with death and fear that we have not tried to imagine what living might be without the pressure of suffering. And the artists have been so busy with the nightmare they have had no time to rewrite the old utopias. All our nobilities are those of the victories over suffering. We are soaked in the grandeur of suffering; and can imagine happiness only as the yawn of a suburban Sunday afternoon.

Yet there have been attempts enough to fill the gap. The literary products of the socialist third of the world can scarcely be said to lack optimism. Anyone who has studied them is familiar with that jolly, jaunty, curiously unemotional novel about the collective farm, the factory, the five-year plan, which is reminiscent of nothing so much as of a little boy whistling in the dark. The simple demand for simple statements of faith produces art so intolerably dull and false that one reads it yawning and returns to Tolstoy.

Meanwhile, the best and most vital works of Western literature have been despairing statements of emotional anarchy. If the typical product of communist literature during the last two decades is the cheerful little tract about economic advance, then the type of Western literature is the novel or play which one sees or reads with a shudder of horrified pity for all of humanity. If writers like Camus, Sartre, Genet, Beckett, feel anything but a tired pity for human beings, then it is not evident from their work.

I believe that the pleasurable luxury of despair, the acceptance of disgust, is as much a betrayal of what a writer should be as the acceptance of the simple economic view of man; both are aspects of cowardice, both fallings-away from a central vision, the two easy escapes of our time into false innocence. They are the opposite sides of the same coin. One sees man as the isolated individual unable to communicate, helpless and solitary; the other as collective man with a collective conscience. Somewhere between these two, I believe, is a resting point, a place of decision, hard to reach and precariously balanced. It is a balance which must be continuously tested and reaffirmed. Living in the midst of this whirlwind of change, it is impossible to make final judgements or absolute statements of value. The point of rest

15

should be the writer's recognition of man, the responsible individual, voluntarily submitting his will to the collective, but never finally; and insisting on making his own personal and private judgements before every act of submission.

I think that a writer who has for many years been emotionally involved in the basic ethical conflict of communism – what is due to the collective and what to the individual conscience – is peculiarly equipped to write of the dangers inherent in being 'committed.' The writer who can be bludgeoned into silence by fear or economic pressure is not worth considering; these problems are simple and the dangers easily recognizable. What is dangerous is the inner loyalty to something felt as something much greater than one's self. I remember, in Moscow, when this question was discussed, a writer replied to an accusation of being bludgeoned by the Party into false writing by saying: 'No one bludgeons us. Our conscience is at the service of the people. We develop an inner censor.' It is the inner censor which is the enemy.

This same attitude was expressed at a higher level during another conversation I had with one of the well-known Soviet writers some months before the Twentieth Congress. He had been telling me about his experiences during the thirties. Because he had refused to inform on some of his colleagues he had suffered two years of what amounted to social ostracism. He was not a communist but he had a deep emotional loyalty to the communist ideals. I asked him if he had written about his experiences, saying that, since Sholokov, there had been many interesting small books produced in Soviet literature, but none describing the great conflict between good and evil which was still being played out in his country. I said I could understand that such books could not be published now, but there would come a time when they would be published. He replied: 'How could I write of that? It was too painful, too difficult to know what was wrong and what was right.' I said that if the people like himself remained silent about this struggle, the literature of his country would be impoverished. He said: 'To write of such suffering, to write of such pain, would need an objectivity proper only to a second-rate writer. A great writer has a warmth of heart which commits him to the deepest pain and suffering of his people. But to step back from that experience far enough to write about it would mean a coldness of heart.' I said that what he was saying amounted to a new theory of art. To which he replied: 'Art can look after itself. Art will always recreate itself in different forms. But there are times when humanity is so pitiful and so exposed that art should be willing to stand aside and wait. Art is arrogant unless it is prepared to stand aside.'

This sums up for me, and where I feel it most deeply and personally, the point where 'committedness' can sell out to expediency. Once you admit that 'art should be willing to stand aside for life,' then the little tracts about progress, the false optimism, the dreadful lifeless products of socialist realism, become inevitable.

People who have been influenced by, or who have lived inside, the communist ethos, will understand the complicated emotions, the difficult loyalties, behind what that Soviet writer said. For me it is depressing that the younger people now have no understanding of it. This is the real gap between people of my age and, to choose a point at random, people under thirty. Rejecting 'propaganda,' for this is what they believe they are doing, they reject an imaginative understanding of what I am convinced is the basic conflict of our time. The mental climate created by the cold war has produced a generation of young intellectuals who totally reject everything communism stands for; they cut themselves off imaginatively from a third of mankind, and impoverish themselves by doing so.

It is this conflict which I am trying to explore in my series of novels, 'Children of Violence,' two volumes of which have appeared. Not one critic has understood what I should have thought would be obvious from the first chapter, where I was at pains to state the theme very clearly: that this is a study of the individual conscience in its relations with the collective. The fact that no critic has seen this does not, of course, surprise me. As long as critics are as 'sensitive,' subjective, and uncommitted to anything but their own private sensibilities, there will be no body of criticism worth taking seriously in this country. At the moment our critics remind me of a lot of Victorian ladies making out their library lists: this is a 'nice' book; or it is not a 'nice' book; the characters are 'nice'; or they are not 'nice.'

What we need more than anything else, I am convinced, is some serious criticism. The most exciting periods of literature have always been those when the critics were great.

We are not living in an exciting literary period but in a dull one. We are not producing masterpieces, but large numbers of small, quite lively, intelligent novels. Above all, current British literature is provincial. This in spite of the emergence of the Angry Young Men. I use the phrase not because I think it is in any way an adequate description but because it is immediately recognizable.

When as a socialist I look forward to the working class being emancipated into readers and writers of serious literature, it is not because I believe books 'about' workers are better than books by or about middle-class people. I make a point of saying this because it is assumed that this is what socialists believe. It is because when a hitherto inarticulate class is released into speech, it brings a fresh rush of vitality into literature. This is why the work of the Angry Young Men was like an injection of vitality into the withered arm of British literature. It expresses something new; a section of the intelligentsia who are scornful of middle-class values; reject The Establishment; are refreshingly derisive and are not prepared to be bullied by phrases like 'good taste.' Yet they are extremely provincial and I do not mean by provincial that they come from or write about the provinces. I mean that their horizons are bounded by their immediate experience of British life and standards.

As an example there is John Braine's book *Room at the Top*, which was compared with Stendhal's work. This comparison exactly pinpoints what I mean. Stendhal's bitterly opportunist heroes sought their various destinies in the painful twilight of the reaction that followed the French Revolution. The grandeur of Stendhal's vision comes precisely from his bitter knowledge of the pettiness of life after a great vision had failed. But the hero of *Room at the Top*, whose values are similar to Stendhal's heroes, who understand, as clearly as Julien Sorel when he is allowing himself to be corrupted, does not see himself in relation to any larger vision. Therefore he remains petty.

It seems to me that the work of all the new younger writers is essentially a protest against the pettiness and narrowness of what is offered them. From Jimmy Porter to Lucky Jim they are saying: 'I am too good for what I am offered.' And so they are.

British life is at the moment petty and frustrating. The people in these islands are kindly, pleasant, tolerant; apparently content to sink into ever-greater depths of genteel poverty because of the insistence of our rulers on spending so much of the wealth we produce on preparations for a war against communism; a war which will take place if and when the United States decides. They are a people who have lost the habit of fighting back; they will emigrate, but they won't rebel, or at least, not about fundamentals. If there is industrial strife, even socialist newspapers behave like anxious maiden aunts, exhorting both sides to play the game and not to step outside the rules of fair play. For the workers are striking because their standard of living is fluctuating, not because a fifth of the products of their work is being spent on armaments which almost at once become obsolete; not because this is a rich country being artificially kept poor. If there is a disciplinary war against a dissident colony, the young men obediently march off, because they have been educated not to think, or because war experience is likely to be the only exciting and interesting experience they can look forward to. The working people get their view of life through a screen of high-pressure advertising; sex-sodden newspapers and debased films and television; the middle classes, from a press which from *The Times* to the *New Statesman* is debilitated by a habit of languid conformity which is attacking Britain like dry rot.

It is a country so profoundly parochial that people like myself, coming in from outside, never cease to marvel. Do the British people know that all over what is politely referred to as the Commonwealth, millions of people continually discuss and speculate about their probable reactions to this or that event? No, and if they did, they would not care. I remember being in the House of Commons one afternoon when some Colonial issue was being discussed. There were more Africans in the Strangers' Gallery than there were Members of Parliament who thought the matter important enough to take their seats in the House. Does the Labour movement understand that hundreds of thousands of the more intelligent people in the Colonies, people whose awakening has very often been fed by the generous age of British literature – poets like Shelley and Byron and Burns, writers like Dickens – look to them for help and guidance? For the most part, socialists are not very interested in what is going on in the Colonies. To discuss politics in Britain with most people means that in five minutes one is astounded to find that the talk is of whether old Freddie or Tony is going to be sent out to govern New South Wales, or whether brother John or Jack will be the next secretary of the Trade Union.

Thinking internationally means choosing a particular shade of half-envious, half-patronizing emotion to feel about the United States; or collecting money for Hungary, or taking little holidays in Europe, or liking French or Italian films.

Meanwhile the world churns, bubbles, and ferments.

All over that enormous land mass, the Soviet Union and China, the most epic movement of change ever known in history is taking place. It is the greatest event of our time, and one in which we are all involved. But, to quote a young intellectual aged about twenty-five: 'All that sort of thing, my dear, is really rather *vieux jeu*, isn't it? I mean to say, progress and all that is rather old hat.'

And the most exciting and interesting writers we are producing in this country, for all their vitality, are sunk inside the parochialism.

Mr Amis, for instance, who says he envies writers who have a cause to inspire them: Colonial freedom, for instance. This is the Victorian charitable view; the poor are always with us, suitable objects for uplifting emotions. For apparently Mr Amis, although a Welshman*, does not see Britain in intimate relation and interaction with other countries. Mr Amis also says that self-interest is the only authentic political motive. Without going into the psychological analysis of motives, which always cuts too many ways to be useful, the fact is that everywhere in the world

*At the original time of writing, I was under the impression that Kingsley Amis was a Welshman. Therefore this comment is absurd.

people with nothing to gain from being socialists (nothing to gain in the sense that Mr Amis uses) have become, are becoming, and will become, socialists of one kind or another. Most of the people I have known during the past fifteen years have devoted themselves to causes against their self-interest. Britain has been supremely a country which fed people into various crusading movements, either at home or abroad, people with nothing to gain but the maintenance of their self-respect. Mr Amis is generalizing from an emotion which is current among a section of his generation now. It is a temporary mood of disillusion.

There is Mr Colin Wilson, who sees no reason why he should not state that: 'Like all my generation I am anti-humanist and anti-materialist.' Mr Wilson has every right to be anti-humanist and anti-materialist; but it is a sign of his invincible British provincialism that he should claim to speak for his generation. The fact is that outside the very small sub-class of humanity Mr Wilson belongs to, vast numbers of young people are both humanist and materialist. Millions of young people in China, the Soviet Union, and India, for instance. And the passions that excite the young African nationalist, five years literate, watching the progress of dams being built in India and China, because he knows that what goes on in other countries intimately affects himself, have little in common with the passions of Mr Wilson. Mr Wilson may find the desire of backward people not to starve, not to remain illiterate, rather uninteresting, but he and people like him should at least try and understand it exists, and what a great and creative force it is, one which will affect us all.

Then there is Mr Osborne, whose work, if I understand it rightly, is a passionate protest against littleness. There are no great causes left to fight for. Jimmy Porter is doomed to futility because he was born too late for the French

Revolution. Admittedly Stendhal exclaimed: 'Happy the heroes who died before 1804,' but that was quite a long time ago. But because other people have done the fighting for Jimmy Porter in the thirties and the forties, there is nothing for it but to stagnate and submit to being sucked dry by women. I think I quote more or less correctly.

But when it reaches the point where we are offered the sex war as a serious substitute for social struggle, even if ironically, then it is time to examine the reasons. That there are no pure causes left? True; but occasions as simply and obviously just as the Storming of the Bastille don't often occur in history. And in the thirties a good deal of passion went into causes complicated by the split in the socialist movement; and in the forties people were prepared to die in order to defend the bad against the worse.

The other day I met a girl who said she envied me because I had had at least ten years of being able to believe in the purity of communism, which advantage was denied to her generation. All of us, she said, were living off the accumulated fat of the socialist hump. She was a socialist herself, but without any enthusiasm.

But what is this socialist hump it seems that we, the middle-aged, are living off? Somebody once said that there was nothing more arrogant than to demand a perfect cause to identify oneself with. It is true that when I became a communist, emotionally if not organizationally, in 1942, my picture of socialism as developed in the Soviet Union was, to say the least, inaccurate. But after fifteen years of uncomfortable adjustment to reality I still find myself in the possession of an optimism about the future obviously considered jejune by anyone under the age of thirty. (In Britain, that is.) Perhaps it is that the result of having been a communist is to be a humanist.

For a while I imagined that the key to this disillusionment

might be found by comparing our time with the disillusionment which followed the French Revolution. To this end I reread Stendhal. 'Injustice and absurdity still made him angry in spite of himself, and he was still angrier at being so, and at taking an interest in that absurd and rascally mob which forms the immense majority of mankind.' 'It is the party spirit,' replied Altamira. 'There are no longer any genuine passions in the nineteenth century; that is why people are so bored in France. We commit the greatest cruelties, but without cruelty.' Such remarks seem contemporary enough.

Yet we are all of us, directly or indirectly, caught up in a great whirlwind of change; and I believe that if an artist has once felt this, in himself, and felt himself as part of it; if he has once made the effort of imagination necessary to comprehend it, it is an end of despair, and the aridity of self-pity. It is the beginning of something else which I think is the minimum act of humility for a writer: to know that one is a writer at all because one represents, makes articulate, is continuously and invisibly fed by, numbers of people who are inarticulate, to whom one belongs, to whom one is responsible.

Because this is not a great age of literature it is easy to fall into despondency and frustration. For a time I was depressed because I thought it likely that the novel might very well be on the way out altogether. It was, after all, born with the middle class, and might die with the middle class. A hundred years ago people used to wait impatiently for the next instalment of a novel. Cinema and television have been added to the popular arts, where once the novel was alone.

But the novelist has one advantage denied to any of the other artists. The novel is the only popular art-form left where the artist speaks directly, in clear words, to his audience. Film-makers, playwrights, television writers, have to reach people through a barrier of financiers, actors, producers, directors. The novelist talks, as an individual to individuals, in a small personal voice. In an age of committee art, public art, people may begin to feel again a need for the small personal voice; and this will feed confidence into writers and, with confidence because of the knowledge of being needed, the warmth and humanity and love of people which is essential for a great age of literature.

Preface to
The Golden Notebook

The shape of this novel is as follows:

There is a skeleton, or frame, called *Free Women*, which is a conventional short novel, about 60,000 words long, and which could stand by itself. But it is divided into five sections and separated by stages of the four Notebooks, Black, Red, Yellow, and Blue. The Notebooks are kept by Anna Wulf, a central character of *Free Women*. She keeps four and not one because, as she recognizes, she has to separate things off from each other, out of fear of chaos, of formlessness – of breakdown. Pressures, inner and outer, end the Notebooks; a heavy black line is drawn across the page of one after another. But now that they are finished, from their fragments can come something new, *The Golden Notebook*.

Throughout the Notebooks people have discussed, theorized, dogmatized, labelled, compartmented – sometimes in voices so general and representative of the time that they are anonymous, you could put names to them like those in the old Morality Plays, Mr Dogma and Mr I-Am-Free-Because-I-Belong-Nowhere, Miss I-Must-Have-Love-and Happiness and Mrs I-Have-to-Be-Good-at-Everything-I-Do, Mr Where-Is-a-Real-Woman? and Miss Where-Is-a-Real-Man?, Mr I'm-Mad-Because-They-Say-I-Am, and Miss Life-Through-Experiencing-Everything, Mr I-Make Revolution-and-Therefore-I-Am and Mr and Mrs If-We-Deal-Very-Well-with-This-Small-Problem-Then-Perhaps-We-Can-Forget-

We-Daren't-Look-at-the-Big-Ones. But they have also reflected each other, been aspects of each other, given birth to each other's thoughts and behaviour – *are* each other, form wholes. In the inner Golden Notebook, things have come together, the divisions have broken down, there is formlessness with the end of fragmentation – the triumph of the second theme, which is that of unity. Anna and Saul Green the American 'break down.' They are crazy, lunatic, mad – what you will. They 'break down' into each other, into other people, break through the false patterns they have made of their pasts, the patterns and formulas they have made to shore up themselves and each other, dissolve. They hear each other's thoughts, recognize each other in themselves. Saul Green, the man who has been envious and destructive of Anna, now supports her, advises her, gives her the theme for her next book, *Free Women* – an ironical title, which begins: 'The two women were alone in the London flat.' And Anna, who has been jealous of Saul to the point of insanity, possessive and demanding, gives Saul the pretty new notebook, *The Golden Notebook*, which she has previously refused to do, gives him the theme for his next book, writing in it the first sentence: 'On a dry hillside in Algeria a soldier watched the moonlight glinting on his rifle.' In the inner Golden Notebook, which is written by both of them, you can no longer distinguish between what is Saul and what is Anna, and between them and the other people in the book.

This theme of 'breakdown', that sometimes when people 'crack up' it is a way of self-healing, of the inner self's dismissing false dichotomies and divisions, has of course been written about by other people, as well as by me, since then. But this is where, apart from the odd short story, I first wrote about it. Here it is rougher, more close to experience, before experience has shaped itself into thought and pattern – more valuable perhaps because it is rawer material.

But nobody so much as noticed this central theme, because the book was instantly belittled, by friendly reviewers as well as by hostile ones, as being about the sex war, or was claimed by women as a useful weapon in the sex war.

I have been in a false position ever since, for the last thing I have wanted to do was to refuse to support women.

To get the subject of Women's Liberation over with – I support it, of course, because women are second-class citizens, as they are saying energetically and competently in many countries. It can be said that they are succeeding, if only to the extent they are being seriously listened to. All kinds of people previously hostile or indifferent say: 'I support their aims but I don't like their shrill voices and their nasty ill-mannered ways.' This is an inevitable and easily recognizable stage in every revolutionary movement: reformers must expect to be disowned by those who are only too happy to enjoy what has been won for them. I don't think that Women's Liberation will change much, though – not because there is anything wrong with their aims but because it is already clear that the whole world is being shaken into a new pattern by the cataclysms we are living through; probably by the time we are through, if we do get through at all, the aims of Women's Liberation will look very small and quaint.

But this novel was not a trumpet for Women's Liberation. It described many female emotions of aggression, hostility, resentment. It put them into print. Apparently what many women were thinking, feeling, experiencing, came as a great surprise. Instantly a lot of very ancient weapons were unleashed, the main ones, as usual, being on the theme of 'She is unfeminine,' 'She is a man-hater.' This particular reflex seems indestructible. Men – and many women – said that the suffragettes were defeminized, masculine, brutalized. There is no record I have read of any society anywhere when women demanded more than nature offers them that does not also describe this reaction from men – and some women. A lot of women were angry about *The Golden Notebook*. What women will say to other women, grumbling in their kitchens and complaining and gossiping or what they make clear in their masochism, is often the last thing they will say aloud – a man may overhear. Women are the cowards they are because they have been semi-slaves for so long. The number of women prepared to stand up for what they really think, feel, experience with a man they are in love with is still small. Most women will still run like little dogs with stones thrown at them when a man says: You are unfeminine, aggressive, you are unmanning me. It is my belief that any woman who marries or takes seriously in any way at all, a man who uses this threat, deserves everything she gets. For such a man is a bully, does not know anything about the world he lives in, or about its history – men and women have taken infinite numbers of roles in the past, and do now, in different societies. So he is ignorant, or fearful about being out of step – a coward . . . I write all these remarks with exactly the same feeling as if I were writing a letter to post into the distant past: I am so sure that everything we now take for granted is going to be utterly swept away in the next decade.

(So why write novels? Indeed, why! I suppose we have to go on living *as if* . . .)

Some books are not read in the right way because they have skipped a stage of opinion, assume a crystallization of information in society which has not yet taken place. This book was written as if the attitudes that have been created by the Women's Liberation movements already existed. It came out first ten years ago, in 1962. If it were coming out now for the first time it might be read, and not merely reacted to: things have changed very fast. Certain hypocrisies have gone. For instance, ten, or even five years ago – it has been a sexually contumacious time – novels and plays were being plentifully written by men furiously critical of women – particularly from the States but also in this country – portrayed as bullies and betrayers, but particularly as underminers and sappers. But these attitudes in male writers were taken for granted, accepted as sound philosophical bases, as quite normal, certainly not as woman-hating, aggressive, or neurotic. It still goes on, of course, but things are better, there is no doubt of it.

I was so immersed in writing this book that I didn't think about how it might be received. I was involved not merely because it was hard to write – keeping the plan of it in my head I wrote it from start to end, consecutively, and it was difficult – but because of what I was learning as I wrote. Perhaps giving oneself a tight structure, making limitations for oneself, squeezes out new substance where you least expect it. All sorts of ideas and experiences I didn't recognize as mine emerged when writing. The actual time of writing, then, and not only the experiences that had gone into the writing, was really traumatic: it changed me. Emerging from this crystallizing process, handing the manuscript to publisher and friends, I learned that I had written a tract about the sex war, and fast discovered that nothing I said then could change that diagnosis.

Yet the essence of the book, the organisation of it, everything in it, says implicitly and explicitly, that we must not divide things off, must not compartmentalize.

'Bound. Free. Good. Bad. Yes. No. Capitalism. Socialism. Sex. Love . . .' says Anna, in *Free Women*, stating a theme – shouting it, announcing a motif with drums and fanfares . . . or so I imagined. Just as I believed that in a book called *The Golden Notebook* the inner section called the Golden Notebook might be presumed to be a central point, to carry the weight of the thing, to make a statement.

But no.

Other themes went into the making of this book, which was a crucial time for me: thoughts and themes I had been holding in my mind for years came together.

One was that it was not possible to find a novel which described the intellectual and moral climate of a hundred years ago, in the middle of the last century, in Britain, in the way Tolstoy did it for Russia, Stendhal for France. (At this point it is necessary to make the obligatory disclaimers.) To read *The Red and the Black* and *Lucien Leuwen* is to know that France as if one were living there, to read *Anna Karenina* is to know that Russia. But a very useful Victorian novel never got itself written. Hardy tells us what it was like to be poor, to have an imagination larger than the possibilities of a very narrow time, to be a victim. George Eliot is good as far as she goes. But I think the penalty she paid for being a Victorian woman was that she had to be shown to be a good woman even when she wasn't according to the hypocrisies of the time – there is a great deal she does not understand because she is moral. Meredith, that astonishingly underrated writer, is perhaps nearest. Trollope tried the subject but lacked the scope. There isn't one novel that has the vigour and conflict of ideas in action that is in a good biography of William Morris.

Of course this attempt on my part assumed that that filter which is a woman's way of looking at life has the same validity as the filter which is a man's way. Setting that problem aside, or rather, not even considering it, I decided that to give the ideological 'feel' of our mid-century, it would have to be set among socialists and marxists, because it has been inside the various chapters of socialism that the great debates of our time have gone on; the movements, the wars, the revolutions, have been seen by their participants as movements of various kinds of socialism, or marxism, in advance, containment, or retreat. (I think we should at least concede the possibility that people looking back on our time may see it not at all as we do – just as we, looking back on the English, the French, or even the Russian Revolutions see them differently from the people living then.) But 'Marxism' and its various offshoots, has fermented ideas everywhere, and so fast and energetically that, once 'way out' it has already been absorbed, has become part of ordinary thinking. Ideas that were confined to the far left thirty or forty years ago had pervaded the left generally twenty years ago, and have provided the commonplaces of conventional social thought from right to left for the last ten years. Something so thoroughly absorbed is finished as a force – but it was dominant, and in a novel of the sort I was trying to do had to be central.

Another thought that I had played with for a long time was that a main character should be some sort of an artist, but with a 'block.' This was because the theme of the artist has been dominant in art for some time – the painter, writer, musician – as exemplar. Every major writer has used it, and most minor ones. Those archetypes, the artist and his mirror image the businessman, have straddled our culture, one shown as a boorish insensitive, the other as a creator with all excesses of sensibility and suffering and a towering egotism which has to be forgiven because of his products – in exactly the same way, of course, as the businessman has to be forgiven for the sake of his. We get used to what we have and forget that the artist-as-exemplar is a new theme. Heroes a hundred years ago weren't often artists. They were soldiers and empire builders and explorers and clergymen and politicians – too bad about women, who had scarcely succeeded in becoming Florence Nightingale yet. Only oddballs and eccentrics wanted to be artists, and had to fight for it. But to use this theme of our time 'the artist,' 'the writer,' I decided it would have to be developed by giving the creature a block and discussing the reasons for the block. These would have to be linked with the disparity between the overwhelming problems of war, famine, poverty, and the tiny individual who was trying to mirror them. But what was intolerable, what really could not be borne any longer, was this monstrously isolated, monstrously narcissistic pedestalled paragon. It seems that in their own way the young have seen this and changed it, creating a culture of their own in which hundreds and thousands of people make films, assist in making films, make newspapers of all sorts, make music, paint pictures, write books, take photographs. They have abolished that isolated, creative, sensitive figure – by copying him in hundreds of thousands. A trend has reached an extreme, its conclusion, and so there will be a reaction of some sort, as always happens.

The theme of 'the artist' had to relate to another: subjectivity. When I began writing there was pressure on writers not to be 'subjective.' This pressure began inside communist movements, as a development of the social literary criticism developed in Russia in the nineteenth century, by a group of remarkable talents, of whom Belinsky was the best known, using the arts and particularly literature in the battle against csarism and oppression. It spread fast everywhere, finding an echo as late as the fifties, in this country, with the theme of 'commitment.' It is still potent in communist countries. 'Bothering about your stupid personal concerns when Rome is burning' is how it tends to get itself expressed on the level of ordinary life – and was hard to withstand, coming from one's nearest and dearest, and from people doing everything one respected most: like, for instance, trying to fight colour prejudice in Southern Africa. Yet all the time novels, stories, art of every sort, became more and more personal. In the Blue Notebook, Anna writes of lectures she has been giving: "Art during the Middle Ages was communal, unindividual; it came out of a group consciousness. It was without the driving painful individuality of the art of the bourgeois era. And one day we will leave behind the driving egotism of individual art. We will return to an art which will express not man's self-divisions and separateness from his fellows but his responsibility for his fellows and his brotherhood. Art from the West becomes more and more a shriek of torment recording pain. Pain is becoming our deepest reality . . ." I have been saying something like this. About three months ago, in the middle of this lecture, I began to stammer and couldn't finish . . .'

Anna's stammer was because she was evading something. Once a pressure or a current has started, there is no way of avoiding it: there was no way of *not* being intensely subjective: it was, if you like, the writer's task for that time. You couldn't ignore it: you couldn't write a book about the building of a bridge or a dam and not develop the mind and feelings of the people who built it. (You think this is a caricature? – Not at all. This *either/or* is at the heart of literary criticism in communist countries at this moment.) At last I understood that the way over, or through, this dilemma, the unease at writing about 'petty personal problems,' was to recognize that nothing is personal in the sense that it is uniquely one's own. Writing about oneself, one is writing about others, since your problems, pains, pleasures, emotions – and your extraordinary and remark-able ideas – can't be yours alone. The way to deal with the problem of 'subjectivity,' that shocking business of being preoccupied with the tiny individual who is at the same time caught up in such an explosion of terrible and marvellous possibilities, is to see him as a microcosm and in this way to break through the personal, the subjective, making the personal general, as indeed life always does, transforming a private experience – or so you think of it when still a child, '*I am falling in love*,' '*I am feeling this or that emotion, or thinking that or the other thought*' – into something much larger: growing up is after all only the understanding that one's unique and incredible experience is what everyone shares.

Another idea was that if the book were shaped in the right way it would make its own comment about the conventional novel: the debate about the novel has been going on since the novel was born, and is not, as one would imagine from reading contemporary academics, something recent. To put the short novel *Free Women* as a summary and condensation of all that mass of material, was to say something about the conventional novel, another way of describing the dissatisfaction of a writer when something is finished: How little I have managed to say of the truth, how little I have caught of all that complexity; how can this small neat thing be true when what I experienced was so rough and apparently formless and unshaped.'

But my major aim was to shape a book which would make its own comment, a wordless statement: to talk through the way it was shaped.

As I have said, this was not noticed.

One reason for this is that the book is more in the European tradition than the English tradition of the novel. Or rather, in the English tradition as viewed at the moment. The English novel after all does include *Clarissa* and *Tristram Shandy*, *The Tragic Comedians* – and Joseph Conrad.

But there is no doubt that to attempt a novel of ideas is to give oneself a handicap: the parochialism of our culture is intense. For instance, decade after decade bright young men and women emerge from their universities able to say proudly: 'Of course I know nothing about German literature.' It is the mode. The Victorians knew everything about German literature, but were able with a clear conscience not to know much about the French.

As for the rest – well, it is no accident that I got intelligent criticism from people who were, or who had been, marxists. They saw what I was trying to do. This is because marxism looks at things as a whole and in relation to each other – or tries to, but its limitations are not the point for the moment. A person who has been influenced by marxism takes it for granted that an event in Siberia will affect one in Botswana. I think it is possible that marxism was the first attempt, for our time, outside the formal religions, at a world-mind, a world ethic. It went wrong, could not prevent itself from dividing and subdividing, like all the other religions, into smaller and smaller chapels, sects, and creeds. But it was an attempt.

This business of seeing what I was trying to do – it brings me to the critics, and the danger of evoking a yawn. This sad bickering between writers and critics, playwrights and critics: the public have got so used to it they think, as of quarrelling children: 'Ah yes, dear little things, they are at it again.' Or: 'You writers get all that praise, or if not praise, at least all that attention – so why are you so perennially wounded?' And the public are quite right. For reasons I won't go into here, early and valuable experiences in my writing life gave me a sense of perspective about critics and reviewers; but over this novel, *The Golden Notebook*, I lost it: I thought that for the most part the criticism was too silly to be true. Recovering balance, I understood the problem. It is that writers are looking to the critics for an *alter ego*, that other self more intelligent than oneself who has seen what you are reaching for, and who judges you only by whether you have matched up to your aim or not. I have never yet met a writer who, faced at last with that rare being, a real critic, doesn't lose all paranoia and become gratefully attentive – he has found what he thinks he needs. But what he, the writer, is asking is impossible. Why should he expect this extraordinary being, the perfect critic (who does occasionally exist), why should there be anyone else who comprehends what he is trying to do? After all, there is only one person spinning that particular cocoon, only one person whose business it is to spin it.

It is not possible for reviewers and critics to provide what they purport to provide – and for which writers so ridiculously and childishly yearn.

This is because the critics are not educated for it; their training is in the opposite direction.

It starts when the child is as young as five or six, when he arrives at school. It starts with marks, rewards, 'places,' 'streams,' stars – and still in many places, stripes. This horserace mentality, the victor and loser way of thinking, leads to 'Writer X is, is not, a few paces ahead of Writer Y. Writer Y has fallen behind. In his last book Writer Z has shown himself as better than Writer A.' From the very beginning the child is trained to think in this way: always in terms of comparison, of success, and of failure. It is a weeding-out system: the weaker get discouraged and fall out; a system designed to produce a few winners who are always in competition with each other. It is my belief – though this is not the place to develop this – that the talents every child has, regardless of his official 'I.Q.', could stay with him through life, to enrich him and everybody else, if these talents were not regarded as commodities with a value in the success-stakes.

The other thing taught from the start is to distrust one's own judgement. Children are taught submission to authority, how to search for other people's opinions and decisions, and how to quote and comply.

As in the political sphere, the child is taught that he is free, a democrat, with a free will and a free mind, lives in a free country, makes his own decisions. At the same time he is a prisoner of the assumptions and dogmas of his time, which he does not question, because he has never been told they exist. By the time a young person has reached the age when he has to choose (we still take it for granted that a choice is inevitable) between the arts and the sciences, he often chooses the arts because he feels that here is humanity, freedom, choice. He does not know that he is already moulded by a system: he does not know that the choice itself is the result of a false dichotomy rooted in the heart of our culture. Those who do sense this, and who don't wish to subject themselves to further moulding, tend to leave, in a half-unconscious, instinctive attempt to find work where they won't be divided against themselves. With all our institutions, from the police force to academia, from medicine to politics, we give little attention to the people who leave – that process of elimination that goes on all the time and which excludes, very early, those likely to be original and reforming, leaving those attracted to a thing because that is what they are already like. A young policeman leaves the force saying he doesn't like what he has to do. A young teacher leaves teaching, her idealism snubbed. This social mechanism goes almost unnoticed – yet it is as powerful as any in keeping our institutions rigid and oppressive.

These children who have spent years inside the training system become critics and reviewers, and cannot give what the author, the artist, so foolishly looks for – imaginative and original judgement. What they can do, and what they do very well, is to tell the writer how the book or play accords with current patterns of feeling and thinking – the climate of opinion. They are like litmus paper. They are wind gauges – invaluable. They are the most sensitive of barometers of public opinion. You can see changes of mood and opinion here sooner than anywhere except in the political field. It is because these are people whose whole education has been just that – to look outside themselves for their opinions, to adapt themselves to authority figures, to 'received opinion' – a marvellously revealing phrase.

It may be that there is no other way of educating people. Possibly, but I don't believe it. In the meantime it would be a help at least to describe things properly, to call things by their right names. Ideally, what should be said to every child, repeatedly, throughout his or her school life is something like this:

'You are in the process of being indoctrinated. We have not yet evolved a system of education that is not a system of indoctrination. We are sorry, but it is the best we can do. What you are being taught here is an amalgam of current prejudice and the choice of this particular culture. The slightest look at history will show how impermanent these must be. You are being taught by people who have been able to accommodate themselves to a regime of thought laid down by their predecessors. It is a self-perpetuating system. Those of you who are more robust and individual than others, will be encouraged to leave and find ways of educating yourself – educating your own judgement. Those who stay must remember, always and all the time, that they are being moulded and patterned to fit into the narrow and particular needs of this particular society.'

Like every other writer I get letters all the time from young people who are about to write theses and essays about my books in various countries – but particularly in the United States. They all say: 'Please give me a list of the articles about your work, the critics who have written about you, the authorities.' They also ask for a thousand details of total irrelevance, but which they have been taught to consider important, amounting to a dossier, like an immigration department's.

These requests I answer as follows: 'Dear Student. You are mad. Why spend months and years writing thousands of words about one book, or even one writer, when there are hundreds of books waiting to be read. You don't see that you are the victim of a pernicious system. And if you have yourself chosen my work as your subject, and if you do have to write a thesis – and believe me I am very grateful that what I've written is being found useful by you – then why don't you read what I have written and make up your own mind about what you think, testing it against your own life, your own experience. Never mind about Professors White and Black.'

'Dear Writer' – they reply. 'But I have to know what the authorities say, because if I don't quote them, my professor won't give me any marks.'

This is an international system, absolutely identical from the Urals to Yugoslavia, from Minnesota to Manchester.

The point is, we are so used to it, we no longer see how bad it is.

I am not used to it, because I left school when I was fourteen. There was a time I was sorry about this, and believed I had missed out on something valuable. Now I am grateful for a lucky escape. After the publication of *The Golden Notebook*, I made it my business to find out something about the literary machinery, to examine the process which made a critic, or a reviewer. I looked at innumerable examination papers – and couldn't believe my eyes; sat in on classes for teaching literature, and couldn't believe my ears.

You might be saying: That is an exaggerated reaction, and you have no right to it, because you say you have never been part of the system. But I think it is not all exaggerated, and that the reaction of someone from outside is valuable simply because it is fresh and not biased by allegiance to a particular education.

But after this investigation, I had no difficulty in answering my own questions: Why are they so parochial, so personal, so small-minded? Why do they always atomize, and belittle, why are they so fascinated by detail and uninterested in the whole? Why is their interpretation of the word *critic* always to find fault? Why are they always seeing writers as in conflict with each other, rather than complementing each other? Simple, this is how they are trained to think. That valuable person who understands what you are doing, what you are aiming for, and can give you advice and real criticism, is nearly always someone right outside the literary machine, even outside the university system; it may be a student just beginning, and still in love with literature, or perhaps it may be a thoughtful person who reads a great deal, following his own instinct.

I say to these students who have to spend a year, two years, writing theses about one book: 'There is only one way to read, which is to browse in libraries and bookshops, picking up books that attract you, reading only those, dropping them when they bore you, skipping the parts that drag – and never, never reading anything because you feel you ought, or because it is part of a trend or a movement. Remember that the book which bores you when you are twenty or thirty will open doors for you when you are forty or fifty – and vice versa. Don't read a book out of its right time for you. Remember that for all the books we have in print, there are as many that have never reached print, have never been written down. Even now, in this age of compulsive reverence for the written word, history, even social ethic, are taught by means of stories, and the people who have been conditioned into thinking only in terms of what is written – and unfortunately nearly all the products of our educational system can do no more than this – are missing what is before their eyes. For instance, the real history of Africa is still in the custody of black storytellers and wise men and women, black historians, medicine men: it is a verbal history, still kept safe from the white man and his predations. Everywhere, if you keep your mind open, you will find the truth in words *not* written down. So never let the printed page be your master. Above all, you should know that the fact that you have to spend one year or two years on one book, or one author, means that you are badly taught – you should have been taught to read your way from one sympathy to another, you should be learning to follow your own intuitive feeling about what you need: that is what you should have been developing, not the way to quote from other people.'

But unfortunately it is nearly always too late.

It did look for a while as if the recent student rebellions might change things, as if the students' impatience with the dead stuff they are taught might be strong enough to substitute something more fresh and useful. But it seems as if the rebellion is over. Sad. During the lively time in the States, I had letters with accounts of how classes of students had refused their syllabuses, and were bringing to class their own choice of books, those that they had found relevant to their lives. The classes were emotional, sometimes violent, angry, exciting, sizzling with life. Of course this only happened with teachers who were sympathetic, and prepared to stand with the students against authority – prepared for the consequences. There are teachers who know that the way they have to teach is bad and boring. Luckily there are still enough, with a bit of luck, to overthrow what is wrong, even if the students themselves have lost impetus.

Meanwhile there is a country . . .

* * *

Where thirty or forty years ago, a critic made a private list of writers and poets which he, personally, considered made up what was valuable in literature, dismissing all others. This list he defended lengthily in print, for The List instantly became a subject for much debate. Millions of words were written for and against – schools and sects, for and against, came into being. The argument, all these years later, still continues . . . No one finds this state of affairs sad or ridiculous . . .

Where there are critical books of immense complexity and learning, dealing, but often at second or third hand, with original work – novels, plays, stories. The people who write these books form a stratum in universities across the world – they are an international phenomenon, the top layer of literary academia. Their lives are spent in criticizing, and in criticizing each other's criticism. They at least regard this activity as more important than the original work. It is possible for literary students to spend more time reading criticism and criticism of criticism than they spend reading poetry, novels, biography, stories. A great many people regard this state of affairs as quite normal, and not sad and ridiculous . . .

Where I recently read an essay about *Antony and Cleopatra* by a boy shortly to take A levels. It was full of originality and excitement about the play, the feeling that any real teaching about literature aims to produce. The essay was returned by the teacher like this: 'I cannot mark this essay, you haven't quoted from the authorities.' Few teachers would regard this as sad and ridiculous . . .

Where people who consider themselves educated, and indeed as superior to and more refined than ordinary nonreading people, will come up to a writer and congratulate him or her on getting a good review somewhere but will not consider it necessary to read the book in question, or ever to think that what they are interested in is success . . .

Where when a book comes out on a certain subject, let's say star-gazing, instantly a dozen colleges, societies, television programmes, write to the author asking him to come and speak about star-gazing. The last thing it occurs to them to do is to read the book. This behaviour is considered quite normal, and not ridiculous at all . . .

Where a young man or woman, reviewer, or critic, who has not read more of a writer's work than the book in front of him, will write patronizingly, or as if rather bored with the whole business, or as if considering how many marks to give an essay, about the writer in question – who might have written fifteen books, and have been writing for twenty or thirty years – giving the said writer instruction on what to write next, and how. No one thinks this is absurd, certainly not the young person, critic, or reviewer, who has been taught to patronize and itemize everyone for years, from Shakespeare downwards.

Where a Professor of Archaeology can write of a South American tribe which has advanced knowledge of plants, and of medicine and of psychological methods: 'The astonishing thing is that these people have no written language . . .' And no one thinks him absurd.

Where, on the occasion of a centenary of Shelley, in the same week and in three different literary periodicals, three young men, of identical education, from our identical universities, can write critical pieces about Shelley, damning him with the faintest possible praise and in identically the same tone, as if they were doing Shelley a great favour to mention him at all – and no one seems to think that such a thing can indicate that there is something seriously wrong with our literary system.

Finally . . . this novel continues to be, for its author, a most instructive experience. For instance. Ten years after I wrote it, I can get, in one week, three letters about it, from three intelligent, well-informed, concerned people, who have taken the trouble to sit down and write to me. One might be in Johannesburg, one in San Francisco, one in Budapest. And here I sit, in London, reading them, at the same time, or one after another – as always, grateful to the writers, and delighted that what I've written can stimulate, illuminate, or even annoy. But one letter is entirely about the sex war, about man's inhumanity to woman, and woman's in-humanity to man, and the writer has produced pages and pages all about nothing else, for she – but not always a she – can't see anything else in the book.

The second is about politics, probably from an old Red like myself, and he or she writes many pages about politics, and never mentions any other theme.

These two letters used, when the book was as it were young, to be the most common.

The third letter, once rare but now catching up on the others, is written by a man or a woman who can see nothing in it but the theme of mental illness.

But it is the same book.

And naturally these incidents bring up again questions of what people see when they read a book, and why one person sees one pattern and nothing at all of another pattern, and how odd it is to have, as author, such a clear picture of a book that is seen so very differently by its readers.

And from this kind of thought has emerged a new conclusion: which is that it is not only childish of a writer to want readers to see what he sees, to understand the shape and aim of a novel as he sees it, but his wanting this means that he has not understood a most fundamental point. Which is that the book is alive and potent and fructifying and able to promote thought and discussion only when its plan and shape and intention are not understood, because that moment of seeing the shape and plan and intention is also the moment when there isn't anything more to be got out of it.

And when a book's pattern and the shape of its inner life is as plain to the reader as it is to the author, then perhaps it is time to throw the book aside, as having had its day, and start again on something new.

Interview with Doris Lessing

BY ROY NEWQUIST

N. In *A Man and Two Women* the enormous talent of Doris Lessing can be seen in full bloom. Few writers dig to the emotional heart of human involvement better than Miss Lessing, and several critics have observed, in one phrase or another, Miss Lessing's almost uncanny grasp of human relationships: the actual, the artificial, and above all, her command of the vast area where the real and the contrived are blended into the bulk of our lives. To go back to the beginning of things I'll ask Miss Lessing where she was born, reared, and educated.

LESSING: I was born in Persia because my father was running a bank there. He was in Persia because he was fed up with England. He found it too narrow after World War I. Unfortunately, I remember little about Persia consciously – though recently, under mescaline, I found that I remembered a great deal, that it had influenced me without my knowing it.

Then my father went to Southern Rhodesia on an impulse (which is how he ran his life), to farm. He had never been a farmer, but he took a very large tract of land – thousands of acres, in American terms – to grow maize. Thus I was brought up in a district that was populated sparsely, very sparsely indeed, by Scottish people who had left Scotland or England because it was too small for them. I spent most of my childhood alone in a landscape with very few human things to dot it. It was sometimes hellishly lonely, but now I realize how extraordinary it was, and how very lucky I was.

After this I went into town – a very small town that had about ten thousand white persons in it. The black population, of course, did not count, though it was fairly large. I married in my teens, when I was far too young, and had two children. That marriage was a failure and I married again. Let's put it this way: I do not think that marriage is one of my talents. I've been much happier unmarried than married. I can't blame the people I've been married to – by and large I've been at fault.

N. When did you start writing?

LESSING: I think I've always been a writer by temperament. I wrote some bad novels in my teens. I always knew I would be a writer, but not until I was quite old – twenty-six or -seven – did I realize that I'd better stop saying I was *going* to be one and get down to business. I was working in a lawyer's office at the time, and I remember walking in and saying to my boss, 'I'm giving up my job because I'm going to write a novel.' He very properly laughed, and I indignantly walked home and wrote *The Grass Is Singing*. I'm oversimplifying; I didn't write it as simply as that because I was clumsy at writing and it was much too long, but I did learn by writing it. It focused upon white people in Southern Rhodesia, but it could have been about white people anywhere south of the Zambezi, white people who were not up to what is expected of them in a society where there is very heavy competition from the black people coming up. Then I wrote short stories set in the district I was brought up in, where very isolated white farmers lived immense distances from each other. You see, in this background, people can spread themselves out.

People who might be extremely ordinary in a society like England's, where people are pressed into conformity, can become wild eccentrics in all kinds of ways they wouldn't dare try elsewhere. This is one of the things I miss, of course, by living in England. I don't think my memory deceives me, but I think there were more colourful people back in Southern Rhodesia because of the space they had to move in. I gather, from reading American literature, that this is the kind of space you have in America in the Midwest and West.

I left Rhodesia and my second marriage to come to England, bringing a son with me. I had very little money, but I've made my living as a professional writer ever since, which is really very hard to do. I had rather hard going, to begin with, which is not a complaint; I gather from my American writer-friends that it is easier to be a writer in England than in America because there is much less pressure put on us. We are not expected to be successful, and it is no sin to be poor.

N. I don't know how we can compare incomes, but in England it seems that writers make more from reviewing and from broadcasts than they can in the United States.

LESSING: I don't know. When I meet American writers, the successful ones, they seem to make more on royalties, but then they also seem to spend much more. I know a writer isn't supposed to talk about money, but it is very important. It is vital for a writer to know how much he can write to please himself, and how much, or little, he must write to earn money. In England you don't have to 'go commercial' if you don't mind being poor. It so happens that I'm not poor any more, thank goodness, because it's not good for anyone to be. Yet there are disadvantages to living in England. It's not an exciting place to live, it is not one of the hubs of the world, like America, or Russia, or China. England is a backwater, and it doesn't make much difference what happens here, or what decisions are made here. But from the point of view of writing, England is a paradise for me.

You see, I was brought up in a country where there is very heavy pressure put on people. In Southern Rhodesia it is not possible to detach yourself from what is going on. This means that you spend all your time in a torment of conscientiousness. In England – I'm not saying it's a perfect society, far from it – you can get on with your work in peace and quiet when you choose to withdraw. For this I'm very grateful – I imagine there are few countries left in the world where you have this right of privacy.

N. This what you're supposed to find in Paris.

LESSING: Paris is too exciting. I find it impossible to work there. I proceed to have a wonderful time and don't write a damn thing.

N. To work from *A Man and Two Women* for a bit. The almost surgical job you do in dissecting people, not bodily, but emotionally, has made me wonder if you choose your characters from real life, form composites or projections, or if they are so involved you can't really trace their origins.

LESSING: I don't know. Some people I write about come out of my life. Some, well, I don't know where they come from. They just spring from my own consciousness, perhaps the subconscious, and I'm surprised as they emerge.

This is one of the excitements about writing. Someone says something, drops a phrase, and later you find that phrase turning into a character in a story, or a single, isolated, insignificant incident becomes the germ of a plot.

N. If you were going to give advice to the young writer, what would that advice be?

LESSING: You should write, first of all, to please yourself. You shouldn't care a damn about anybody else at all. But writing can't be a way of life; the important part of writing is living. You have to live in such a way that your writing emerges from it. This is hard to describe.

N. What about reading as a background ?

LESSING: I've known very good writers who've never read anything. Of course, this is rare.

N. What about your own reading background?

LESSING: Well, because I had this isolated childhood, I read a great deal. There was no one to talk to, so I read. What did I read? The best – the classics of European and American literature. One of the advantages of not being educated was that I didn't have to waste time on the second-best. Slowly, I read these classics. It was my education, and I think it was a very good one.

I could have been educated – formally, that is – but I felt some neurotic rebellion against my parents who wanted me to be brilliant academically. I simply contracted out of the whole thing and educated myself. Of course, there are huge gaps in my education, but I'm nonetheless grateful that it went as it did. One bit of advice I might give the young writer is to get rid of the fear of being thought of as a perfectionist, or to be regarded as pompous. They should strike out for the best, to be the best. God knows we all fall short of our potential, but if we aim very high we're likely to be so much better.

N. How do you view today's literature? and theatre?

LESSING: About theatre, well, I'm very annoyed right now by that phrase 'kitchen sink' that is being used so frequently. I don't think it means very much. There are two kinds of theatre, and I don't think they should be confused. People who want to see a roaring farce, like *Sailor Beware*, should enjoy it. It's perfectly legitimate, and there's nothing wrong with the theatre of entertainment.

The cathartic theatre, theatre that moves people in such a way that they or their lives are changed, or they understand more about themselves, is a totally different thing. The phrase 'kitchen sink' comes from critics who don't know their jobs, or theatregoers who are being bullied into seeing things they don't want to see. They should never go if they don't want to. There's nothing wrong with a minority theatre and a minority literature.

N. What about the recent trend toward introspection?

LESSING: Well, I haven't been to America, but I've met a great many Americans and I think they have a tendency to be much more aware of themselves, and conscious of their society, than we are in Britain (though we're moving that way). By a coincidence I was thinking, this afternoon, about a musical like *West Side Story*, which comes out of a sophisticated society which is very aware of itself. You wouldn't have found in Britain, at the time that was written, a lyric like 'Gee, Officer Krupke.' You have to be very socially self-conscious to write *West Side Story*.

N. What do you feel about the fiction being turned out today? Does it share the same virtues and failings as theatre or can it be considered separately?

LESSING: Quite separately. You want to know what contemporary writers I enjoy reading? The American writers I like, for different reasons, are Malamud and Norman Mailer – even when he's right off centre he lights rockets. And Algren. And that man who wrote *Catch-22*. And of course, Carson McCullers. But I only read the books that drift my way, I don't know everything that comes out.

N. How do you feel about critical reactions to your own works?

LESSING: I don't get my reviews any more. I read reviews if they turn up in the papers I get, but I go through them fast and try to pay little attention to what is said. I think the further I'm removed from this area – reviews, the literary squabble-shop, the better. I got angry over reviews of *The Golden Notebook*. They thought it was personal – it was, in parts. But it was a very highly structured book, carefully planned. The point of that book was the relation of its parts to each other. But the book they tried to turn it into was: The Confessions of Doris Lessing. I remember I went down to my publishers' office to look through the reviews, because they said I'd had a lot of good ones and I should see them. Well I remember thinking: It's surely not possible that all these reviewers should have minds like gossip columnists. Because of the shape of the book, and the point of that shape, and what it meant, they weren't interested.

You see, the literary society in London is very small and incestuous. Everyone knows everyone. The writer who tosses a scrap of autobiography into an otherwise fictional piece (which writers always have done and always will do), he's not credited with any imagination. Everyone says, 'Oh, that character's so and so,' and 'I know that character.' It's all too personal. The standards of criticism are very low. I don't know about American critics, but in this country we have an abysmal standard. Very few writers I know have any respect for the criticism they get. Our attitude is, and has to be, Are the reviews selling reviews or not ? In all other respects, the reviews are humiliating, they are on such a low level and it's all so spiteful and personal.

N. Do reviews sell books in England ?

LESSING: My publishers claim they help build a reputation and that indirectly they do sell books. This is probably true. But in Great Britain everything is much more cumulative and long-term than in America. One simply settles in for what you call the long haul. But 'reputation' – what are reputations worth when they are made by reviewers who are novelists? Writers aren't necessarily good critics. Yet the moment you've written a novel, you're invited to write criticism, because the newspapers like to have one's 'name' on them. One is a 'name' or one is not, you see. Oh, it's very pleasant to be one, I'm not complaining, I enjoy it. But everyone knows that writers tend to be wrong about each other. Look at Thomas Mann and Brecht – they were both towering geniuses, in different ways, and they didn't have any good word for each other.

Ideally we should have critics who are critics and not novelists who need to earn a bit to tide them over, or failed novelists. Is there such an animal, though? Of course, sometimes a fine writer is a good critic, like Lawrence. Look at something that happened last year – I wrote a long article for the *New Statesman* about the mess socialism is in. There was a half-line reference to X. To this day, people say to me, 'that article you wrote attacking X.' This is how people's minds work now. At the first night of one of Wesker's plays, up comes a certain literary figure and says, his voice literally wet with anxiety, 'Oh, Wesker is a much better playwright than Osborne, he is, isn't he?' He felt that someone's grave should be danced on. He was simply tired of voting for Osborne. Tweedledum and Tweedledee. In and out.

You're going to say the literary world has always been like this. But what I said about the theatre earlier applies – nothing wrong with the audience who likes *Who's for Tennis?* and the critics who do. It's all theirs. But they should keep out of the serious theatre. Similarly, of course, the literary world is always going to seethe with people who say, I'm bored with voting for X. But writers should try to keep away from them. Another bit of advice to a young writer – but unfortunately economics make it almost impossible to follow: Don't review, don't go on television, try to keep out of all that. But, of course, if one's broke, and one's asked to review, one reviews. But better not, if possible. Better not go on television, unless there is something serious to be said (and how often is that?). Better to try and remain what we should be – an individual who communicates with other individuals, through the written word.

N. To return to *A Man and Two Women*. Which stories in this collection would you choose as personal favourites ?

LESSING: That's very difficult. I like the first one, titled 'One Off the Short List' because it's so extremely cold and detached – that one's a toughy. I'm pleased that I was able to bring it off the way I did. Then there were a couple of zany stories I'm attached to. The story about incest I liked very much – the one about the brother and the sister who are in love with each other. Not autobiographical at all, actually; perhaps I wish it were. And I like 'To Room 19,' the depressing piece about people who have everything, who are intelligent and educated, who have a home and two or three or four beautiful children, and have few worries, and yet ask themselves 'What for?' This is all too typical of so many Europeans – and, I gather, so many Americans.

N. Perhaps life without challenge or excitement amounts to boredom.

LESSING: Life certainly shouldn't be without excitement. The Lord knows that everything going on at the moment is exciting.

N. But hasn't boredom become one of our most acute social problems?

LESSING: I don't understand people being bored. I find life so enormously exciting all the time. I enjoy everything enormously if only because life is so short. What have I got – another forty years of this extraordinary life – if I'm lucky? But most people live as if they have a weight put on them. Perhaps I'm lucky, because I'm doing what I want all the time, living the kind of life I want to live. I know a great many people, particularly those who are well off and have everything they are supposed to want, who aren't happy.

N. Right now a great many criticisms are levelled against bored Americans who have a surfeit of what they want. Is this true of England ?

LESSING: I think that England is much more of a class society than America. This street I live on is full of very poor people who are totally different from my literary friends. They, in turn, are different from the family I come from, which is ordinary middle class. It isn't simple to describe life in England. For instance, in any given day I can move in five, six different strata or groups. None of them know how other people live, people different from themselves. All these groups and layers and classes have unwritten rules. There are rigid rules for every layer, but they are quite different from the rules in the other groups.

N. Then perhaps you maintain more individuality.

LESSING: The pressures on us all to conform seem to get stronger. We're supposed to buy things and live in ways we don't necessarily want to live. I've seen both forms of oppression, the tyrannical and the subtle. Here in England I can do what I like, think what I like, go where I please. I'm a writer, and I have no boss, so I don't have to conform. Other people have to, though. But in Southern Rhodesia – well, there one can't do or say what one likes. In fact, I'm a prohibited immigrant in South Africa and Central Africa although I lived in Rhodesia twenty-five years. But then, the list of people who are prohibited in these areas is so long now.

I am not as optimistic as I used to be about oppressive societies. When I opened my eyes like a kitten to politics, there were certain soothing clichés about. One was that oppressive societies 'collapsed under their own weight.' Well, the first oppressive society I knew about was South Africa. I lived close to it, and I was told that a society so ugly and brutal could not last. I was told that Franco and his fascist Spain could not last. Here I am, many decades later, and South Africa is worse than it was, Southern Rhodesia is going the same way, and Franco is very much in power. The tyrannical societies are doing very well. I'm afraid that the liberals and certain people on the left tend to be rather romantic about the nature of power.

I'm not comparing tyranny to conformity. The point is that

people who are willing to conform without a struggle, without protest to small things, who will simply forget how to be individuals, can easily be led into tyranny.

N. But isn't there strength in the middle road? In the area that lies between fascism and communism?

LESSING: I don't know. I hope so, but history doesn't give us many successful examples of being able to keep to the middle. Look at the difference between British and American attitudes toward communism right now. Sections of America seem absolutely hypnotized by the kind of propaganda that's fed to them. Now, if it is true that communism is a violent threat to the world, then Britain – which has a different attitude – has been eating and working and sleeping for twenty years without developing ulcers, but America has ulcers. I would say that we are doing a better job of keeping to the middle of the road. You've got some rather pronounced elements who would like to head for the ditch or force a collision. Hasn't America been enfeebled by this hysterical fear of communism? I don't think you sit down to analyse what the word 'communist' means. You end up in the most ridiculous situations, as you did in Cuba. When you see what a great nation like America can do to muddle this Cuban thing you can only shrug your shoulders. Please don't think I'm holding out any brief for my own government, but we're in a lucky position. I mean, England is. We're not very important, but America holds our fortunes in their large and not very subtle hands, and it's frightening. When I went to Russia, in 1952, I came to the not-very-original conclusion that the Americans and Russians were very similar, and that they would like each other 'if.' Now I see you moving closer and beginning to like each other, so now both of you are terrified of the Chinese, who will turn out (given fifteen years and not, I hope, too much bloodshed and misery) to be just like us, also. All of these violent hostilities are unreal. They've got very little to do with human beings.

N. And very little to do with the arts?

LESSING: The arts, nothing! I was talking as a person, not a writer. I spent a great deal of my time being mixed up in politics in one way or another, and God knows what good it ever did. I went on signing things and protesting against things all the while wars were planned and wars were fought. I still do.

N. To get back to your career, what are you working at now?

LESSING: I'm writing volumes four and five of a series I'm calling 'Children of Violence.' I planned this out twelve years ago, and I've finished the first three. The idea is to write about people like myself, people my age who are born out of wars and who have lived through them, the framework of lives in conflict. I think the title explains what I essentially want to say. I want to explain what it is like to be a human being in a century when you open your eyes on war and on human beings disliking other human beings. I was brought up in Central Africa, which means that I was a member of the white minority pitted against a black majority that was abominably treated and still is. I was the daughter of a white farmer who, although he was a very poor man in terms of what he was brought up to expect, could always get loans from the Land Bank which kept him. (I won't say that my father liked what was going on; he didn't.) But he employed anywhere from fifty to one hundred working blacks. An adult black earned twelve shillings a month, rather less than

61

two dollars, and his food was rationed to corn meal and beans and peanuts and a pound of meat per week. It was all grossly unfair, and it's only part of a larger picture of inequity.

One-third of us – one-third of humanity, that is – is adequately housed and fed. Consciously or unconsciously we keep two-thirds of mankind improperly housed and fed. This is what the series of novels is about – this whole pattern of discrimination and tyranny and violence.

N. At the beginning of the interview you mentioned becoming involved with mescaline. Could you describe this in more detail ?

LESSING: I'm not involved with it. I took one dose out of curiosity, and that's enough to be going on with. It was the most extraordinary experience. Lots of different questions arise, but for our purposes the most interesting one is: Who are we? There were several different people, or 'I's' taking part. They must all have been real, genuine, because one has no control over the process once it's under way. I understand that experiences to do with birth are common with people having these drugs. I was both giving birth and being given birth to. Who was the mother, who was the baby? I was both but neither. Several people were talking and in different voices throughout the process – it took three or four hours. Sometimes my mother – odd remarks in my mother's voice, my mother's sort of phrase. Not the kind of thing I say or am conscious of thinking. And the baby was a most philosophic infant, and different from me.

And who stage-managed this thing? Who said there was to be this birth and why? Who, to put it another way, was Mistress of the Ceremony? Looking back, I think that my very healthy psyche decided that my own birth, the one I actually had, was painful and bad (I gather it was, with forceps and much trouble) and so it gave itself a good birth – because the whole of this labour was a progress from misery, pain, unhappiness, toward happiness, acceptance, and the birth 'I' invented for myself was not painful. But what do I mean, we mean, when we say 'my psyche' – or whatever phrase you might use in its place?

And then there's the question of this philosophic baby, a creature who argued steadily with God – I am not a religious person, and 'I' would say I am an atheist. But this baby who was still in the womb did not want to be born. First, there was the war (I was born in 1919) and the smell of war and suffering was everywhere and the most terrible cold. I've never imagined such cold. It was cold because of the war. The baby did not want to be born to those parents (and remember the baby who was also its own mother) and this is the interesting thing, it was bored. Not the kind of boredom described in my story 'To Room 19.' But a sort of cosmic boredom. This baby had been born many times before and the mere idea of 'having to go through it all over again' (a phrase the baby kept using) exhausted it in advance. And it did not want, this very ancient and wise creature, the humiliation of being smothered in white flannel and blue baby ribbons and little yellow ducks. (Incidentally I'll never again be able to touch or look at a baby without remembering that experience, how helpless a baby is, caged in an insipid world of comfort and bland taste and white flannel and too much warmth.) This creature said to God, Yes, I know that boredom is one of the seven deadly sins, but You created me didn't You? Then if You gave me a mind that goes limp with boredom at the experiences You inflict on me, whose fault is it? I'll consent (this baby said) to being born again for the millionth time, if I am given the right to be bored.

But as the birth proceeded, the pain, the boredom, the

cold, the misery (and the smell of war) diminished, until I was born with the sun rising in a glow of firelight.

Yes, but who created all this ? Who made it up ?

It wasn't me, the normal 'I' who conducts her life.

And of course, this question of I, who am I, what different levels there are inside of us, is very relevant to writing, to the process of creative writing about which we know nothing whatsoever. Every writer *feels* when he, she, hits a different level. A certain kind of writing or emotion comes from it. But you don't know who it is who lives there. It is very frightening to write a story like 'To Room 19,' for instance, a story soaked in emotions that you don't recognize as your own.

When I wrote *The Golden Notebook* I deliberately evoked the different levels to write different parts of it. To write the part where two characters are a bit mad, I couldn't do it, I couldn't get to that level. Then I didn't eat for some time by accident (I forgot) and found that there I was, I'd got there. And other parts of *The Golden Notebook* needed to be written by 'I's' from other levels. That is a literary question, a problem to interest writers. But that creature being born wasn't a 'writer.' It was immensely ancient, for a start, and it was neither male nor female, and it had no race or nationality. I can revive the 'feel' or 'taste' of that creature fairly easily. It isn't far off that creature or person you are when you wake up from deep sleep, and for a moment you don't recognize your surroundings and you think: Who am I? Where am I? Is this my hand? You're somebody, all right, but who?

Doris Lessing at Stony Brook:

AN INTERVIEW BY JONAH RASKIN

RASKIN: How did you react to the arrests on campus?

LESSING: I was profoundly shocked. Coming from England, where different assumptions operate, I wasn't prepared for them. Maybe I'm being romantic, but I don't think the English would allow an invasion of university dormitories by the police. Here, police wake students in the middle of the night, cart them off to jail, and no one in the community protests. The knock at five o'clock in the morning is a totalitarian cliché, it's one of the symbols of Soviet police methods, and Nazi police methods; now that cliché is a reality in the United States.

RASKIN: Are the political and cultural movements in the United States very different from those in England?

LESSING: In England people feel they're living in a period of interregnum. They think that something is going to happen, but they don't know what direction it will take or what form it will have. But here it's all absolutely changing. There's no feeling of interregnum.

RASKIN: In the United States political figures, like Jerry Rubin and Abbie Hoffman, have been arrested on charges of possessing drugs. The police have used laws against drugs to

65

harass radicals for their political activities. Is this the case in England ?

LESSING: In England pot isn't associated with politics. The society links the use of drugs with moral degeneracy and with long hair. At first, officials were anxious to convict people who used marijuana. Now they are leaving them alone, but trying, and failing as far as I can determine, to stop the pushers who sell the hard stuff. In England very few people are arrested for pot.

Homosexuals also had difficulty for a long while in England, before the atmosphere changed. For two to three years there was an intense and nasty police persecution of homosexuals. The police prowled in lavatories, made numerous arrests, and got convictions in almost all cases. But middle-class intellectuals, who had become more tolerant of homosexuality, protested, put pressure on the police, and they ceased to persecute homosexuals. For a time homosexuality was still illegal – it's legal now between consenting adults – but because of the shift in public opinion there were no convictions.

RASKIN: Since students all over the world are in rebellion I imagine that English university students have encountered many of the same problems which students here have faced.

LESSING: The arrests at Stony Brook reminded me of a story about the London School of Economics. The college authorities put up gates to control the movements of students who had been demonstrating on campus. The authorities said that the gates were for ornamental purposes, and to promote general efficiency, but the students weren't fooled by their rhetoric. They announced that they were going to break down the gates and then did so. The faculty reacted hysterically. They behaved like a pack of old women, rang up the police, and invited them to the campus to make arrests. The police, who weren't anxious to interfere, took their time coming, and when they finally arrived they made it clear that the teachers would have to inform on their own students. 'Are you prepared to sell out your students?' one policeman asked. The police and the faculty went together to a pub where the radicals were drinking, and one of the professors shouted, 'I am betraying my students. I shall vomit.' He vomited, but he also identified the students to the police, who were then forced to arrest people they wanted to leave undisturbed.

A large proportion of the LSE staff have deliberately sold out their students. A great deal of bitterness exists between staff and students. Occasionally, the British police are intelligent; they try to avoid making unnecessary arrests. But the American police, it seems to me, never indicated one iota of intelligence.

RASKIN: The American police have been extremely violent in the last few years, in the black ghettos, as usual, but also on the campus. They have attacked white middle-class students. People often think that the British bobbie is harmless, docile, but that's a myth isn't it?

LESSING: I can tell you a story about the violent British police, which also indicates the influence of television on politics. Recently, I was at a demonstration in Trafalgar Square. The police had prohibited all groups from demonstrating that day, but a great many people gathered there in violation of the police injunction, determined to go ahead with the rally. It was a peaceful day. The television cameras were out in force. My friends and I asked the cameramen not to leave, because, on the basis of past experience, we have learned that the police will attack demonstrators when the television cameras aren't there. That evening on television there were film clips of the early part of the afternoon, of the crowd sitting in an orderly fashion, of jolly, smiling policemen. That picture is preserved, but the cameras did not capture the violent and ugly scenes which followed. The cops charged the crowd, waded in, and savagely beat demonstrators. There's no record of that. The police act very differently when the television cameras aren't around.

RASKIN: How else has television shaped our lives?

LESSING: Television is probably the biggest social change we've seen in decades. Programmes are churned out day and night, and they are watched in millions of homes. Television has made this planet one world. Young people today are better informed than their parents were, and the new consciousness children have is created largely by television. For one thing, television has a levelling effect; important events are placed side by side with petty incidents.

RASKIN: Yes, you'll see a Viet Cong soldier executed by the Saigon government, and then an advertisement for tooth-paste. The Vietnamese body falls to the ground, the American girl flashes her white teeth.

LESSING: On the news two dozen events of fantastically different importance are announced in exactly the same tone of voice. The voice doesn't discriminate between a divorce, a horse race, a war in the Middle East. The minds of children are profoundly affected. One can read or not read a newspaper, but one cannot not look at the news on television. It's compelling. I know many young people who are as intelligent as I am, but they don't read newspapers. Their sensibility is very different from mine.

RASKIN: I felt that in your most recent novel, *The Four-Gated City*, you wanted to reach out directly to the new audience which has been shaped by television and the atmosphere of violence.

LESSING: I want to reach the youth. Maybe because I was determined to reach people the form of the book has been shot to hell. The first version was too long, and the second time I wrote it the form changed. I've had Children of Violence set up for twenty years. By the time I wrote the last volume I'd put myself into a damned cage, but it's probably better now that I've heaved the rules out. I'm very proud of the form of *The Golden Notebook*.

RASKIN: The form suggests the disintegration of contemporary life, doesn't it?

LESSING: At the beginning of *The Golden Notebook* Anna says, 'the point is, that as far as I can see everything is cracking up.' An epoch of our society, and of socialism, was breaking up at that time. It had been falling apart since the Bomb was dropped on Hiroshima. We didn't know that this was a watershed. It caught us unawares because the Bomb seemed just another ghastly weapon in a long line of ghastly weapons. It was only later that we realized the horror of the event. Slowly, it began to sink into our consciousness, and to this day the shock penetrates deeper and deeper into our minds. Our side used weapons which were more destructive than those of the enemy. I supported England and the USA in the fight against Germany and Japan, but I was nauseated by the bombing of Dresden, and I was disgusted by our own propaganda. I was split down the middle. Throughout my life I've had to support parties, causes, nations, and movements which stink.

RASKIN: You seem to feel that history is a series of explosions.

LESSING: It is. I feel as if the Bomb has gone off inside myself, and in people around me. That's what I mean by the cracking up. It's as if the structure of the mind is being battered from inside. Some terrible new thing is happening. Maybe it'll be marvellous. Who knows ? Today it's hard to distinguish between the marvellous and the terrible.

RASKIN: It's easier to write about corruption and evil than to write about the Good, isn't it?

LESSING: Yes, I know. What is the Good? It's possible that in our time the Good looks terrible. Maybe out of destruction there will be born some new creature. I don't mean physically. What interests me more than anything is how our minds are changing, how our ways of perceiving reality are changing. The substance of life receives shocks all the time, every place, from bombs, from the all-pervasive violence. Inevitably the mind changes.

RASKIN: How do drugs fit into your sense of the changes of the mind ?

LESSING: I took mescaline once. I've taken pot a bit. Drugs give us a glimpse of the future, they extricate us from the cage of time. When people take drugs they discover an unknown part of themselves. When you have to open up, when you're blocked, drugs are useful, but I think it's bad for people to make them a way of life because they become an end in themselves. Pot should be used with caution, but not banned. I'm against all this banning. I think people can expand and explore their minds without using drugs. It demands a great deal of discipline. It's like learning a craft; you have to devote a lot of time, but if you can train yourself to concentrate you can travel great distances.

RASKIN: In your fiction you explore large tracts through dreams, don't you?

LESSING: Dreams have always been important to me. The hidden domain of our mind communicates with us through dreams. I dream a great deal and I scrutinize my dreams. The more I scrutinize the more I dream. When I'm stuck in a book I deliberately dream. I knew a mathematician once who supplied his brain with information and worked it like a computer. I operate in similar way. I fill my brain with the material for a new book, go to sleep, and I usually come up with a dream which resolves the dilemma.

RASKIN: The dreams in *The Golden Notebook* are points of intensity and fusion, aren't they? Anna sees fragments – a lump of earth from Africa, metal from a gun used in Indochina, flesh from people killed in the Korean War, a Communist party badge from someone who died in a Soviet prison – all of which represent crises in contemporary life.

LESSING: The unconscious artist who resides in our depths is a very economical individual. With a few symbols a dream can define the whole of one's life, and warn us of the future, too. Anna's dreams contain the essence of her experience in Africa, her fears of war, her relationship to communism, her dilemma as a writer.

71

RASKIN: Do you think that the Freudian concepts are valid ?

LESSING: There are difficulties about the Freudian land-scape. The Freudians describe the conscious as a small lit area, all white, and the unconscious as a great dark marsh full of monsters. In their view, the monsters reach up, grab you by the ankles, and try to drag you down. But the unconscious can be what you make of it, good or bad, helpful or unhelpful. Our culture has made an enemy of the unconscious. If you mention the word 'unconscious' in a room full of people you see the expressions on their faces change. The word recalls images of dread and threat, but other cultures have accepted the unconscious as a helpful force, and I think we should learn to see it in that way too.

RASKIN: How did you create the character of Mrs Marks, 'Mother Sugar,' in *The Golden Notebook*?

LESSING: My own psychotherapist was somewhat like Mrs Marks. She was everything I disliked. I was then aggressively rational, anti-religious, and a radical. She was Roman Catholic, Jungian, and conservative. It was very upsetting to me at the time, but I found out it didn't matter a damn. I couldn't stand her terminology, but she was a marvellous person. She was one of those rare individuals who know how to help others. If she had used another set of words, if she had talked Freud talk, or aggressive atheism, it wouldn't have made a difference.

RASKIN: In *The Four-Gated City* you speak about art and autobiography. What is the relationship between your fiction and your self ?

LESSING: Since writing *The Golden Notebook* I've become

less personal. I've floated away from the personal. I've stopped saying, 'This is *mine*, this is *my* experience.' Ever since I started writing I've wondered why the artist himself has become a mirror of society. The first novelists didn't write about themselves, but now almost every novelist writes about himself. People are much more interested in the artist as a personality than in the works he creates. Now, when I start writing, the first thing I ask is, 'Who is thinking the same thought? Where are the other people who are like me?' I don't believe any more that I have a thought. There is a thought around.

RASKIN: Do you think that your thoughts are widely shared by others ? Are they representative?

LESSING: For some reason, when you've finished a patch of your life you look back and you see that it has a pattern which you didn't notice when you were living through it. For the last twenty years I have been closely involved with psychiatrists and mentally ill people. I did not make a deliberate choice in the matter, but I started a process which is now common. Twenty years ago it was considered unusual to have a psychiatrist. Now, almost everyone I know has had a breakdown, is in psychoanalysis, or pops in and out of mental hospitals. Mental illness is part of the mainstream. People who are classified as sick are becoming more and more important in England, the USA, and in socialist countries too. People who are called mentally ill are often those who say to the society, 'I'm not going to live according to your rules. I'm not going to conform.' Madness can be a form of rebellion.

RASKIN: You've also been at the centre of many political conflicts. Near the end of *The Golden Notebook* Anna says that '. . . at that moment I sit down to write someone comes into the room, looks over my shoulder and stops me . . . It could be a Chinese peasant. Or one of Castro's guerrilla fighters. Or an Algerian fighting in the FLN. They stand here in the room and they say, why aren't you doing something about us, instead of wasting your time scribbling?' I feel a tension between my life as a writer and my political activity. Could you tell me how you have felt about this situation?

LESSING: I worked in a socialist movement which was sceptical of writers. Anti-intellectualism was rife in Stalin's Russia, and Western communists followed that example and were hostile to intellectuals. They thought writing was inferior to political organizing, that writers should feel ashamed and apologize for writing books. They assumed that all bourgeois writers wrote trash. Active socialists who wanted to write had to make a choice, they had to decide whether they would organize the working class or write books.

I am intensely aware of, and want to write about, politics, but I often find that I am unable to embody my political vision in a novel. I want to write about Chinese peasants, the Algerians in the FLN, but I don't want to present them in false situations. I don't want to leave them out either. I find it difficult to write well about politics. I feel that the writer is obligated to dramatize the political conflicts of his time in his fiction. There is an awful lot of bad socialist literature which presents contemporary history mechanically. I wanted to avoid that pitfall. In the scene from *The Golden Notebook*, which you've mentioned, I was trying to introduce politics and history into Anna's world.

I'm tormented by the inadequacy of the imagination. I've a sense of the conflict between my life as a writer and the terrors of our time. One sits down to write in a quiet flat in

London and one thinks, 'Yes, there's a war going on in Vietnam.' The night before last, when we were having dinner here, the police were raiding the university and arresting students.

RASKIN: How do you view the future?

LESSING: I'm very much concerned about the future. I've been reading a lot of science fiction, and I think that science-fiction writers have captured our culture's sense of the future. *The Four-Gated City* is a prophetic novel. I think it's a true prophecy. I think that the 'iron heel' is going to come down. I believe the future is going to be cataclysmic.

RASKIN: Do you think it is meaningless to talk, using the Maoist vocabulary, of the powers of people over the machine? People of my generation, on the left, are strengthened in their own political actions by the endurance of the Vietnamese and the success of the Cubans against the mighty USA.

LESSING: Vietnam has been bled for years. I have great respect for the Cubans and I hope the Cuban revolution will fulfil its potential. I wish the African revolutions well. But I don't think that what happens in Cuba, in Africa, in Vietnam is very important. The new countries in Africa aren't going to cause nuclear war. I'm not running down heroism. The Cubans and the Vietnamese are heroic, but rather than celebrate their efforts, we should make sure that mankind doesn't destroy itself in the next twenty-five years. I care for what goes on in China, Russia, the USA, wherever the bomb is. I'm impatient with people who emphasize sexual revolution. I say we should all go to bed, shut up about sexual liberation, and go on with the important matters.

We must prevent another major war. We're already in a time of total chaos, but we're so corrupted that we can't see it. The world is rocking. Our values – the commercial values – stink.

RASKIN: You're pessimistic, aren't you? Don't you thin# that my generation has been liberated, and is liberating much of the society? Our values aren't commercial.

LESSING: I'm not saying that the youth have commercial values. In the 1960s the youth have had a great deal of freedom. It has been a wonderful moment in history. During the period of 'flower power' I met some young Canadian poets who assured me that flowers were mightier than tanks. They talked sentimental rubbish. It's too late for romanticism. Young people in this decade have been allowed freedom, they have been flattered and indulged, because they are a new market. Young people coming to the end of this era are hitting exactly what previous generations before them have hit – that awful moment when they see that their lives are going to be, unless they do something fast, like the lives of their parents. The illusion of freedom is destroyed. A large part of the student protest is indirectly due to the fact that after seven or eight years of lotus eating, young people suddenly realize that their lives may be as narrow, as confined, as commercially oriented, as the lives of their parents. They don't want that life, but they feel trapped. This feeling can be good or bad depending how it's used.

RASKIN: You seem to feel that the young are in a dangerous and precarious situation.

LESSING: The important sections of young people are revolutionary. If the atmosphere changes you'll find that the large proportion of students won't be revolutionary. The minority must be safeguarded, because it's the minority which goes on fighting. The last decade has been a brief patch of charming, comparative freedom which is on its way out. The danger is that young people growing up in an era of relative freedom will believe that life has always been, and will continue to be joyful, unrepressive.

RASKIN: But students are already finding out that the society is authoritarian. There are dozens of arrests every day in every city. Students were just arrested at Stony Brook.

LESSING: Yes, that's true, but the fact is that young people are demonstrating and their movement is having an impact on the society. Suppose the situation arises when you and your friends can't demonstrate in public? You should be creating organizations which will survive in a totalitarian state. In the meantime, while you can act openly, you should act openly, and fight for the right to act openly.

RASKIN: Repression is already on its way. In a small way it's affected me.

LESSING: Repression has been very much a part of the history of our time. It has been very difficult to fight openly in the past thirty years. I've seen many opposition movements smashed. Spain has been a fascist country for decades. Portugal is a very efficient fascist state. In the Soviet Union opposition is regularly destroyed. Also, in our time, radicals have been destroyed by their own side. Stalinism destroyed the lives of thousands of people. Every time we have a war, liberties go to hell. In the meantime we go on battling. I'm concerned with the preservation of liberties. I realize that to you that sounds like an old-fashioned liberal bleat, but I've seen liberties destroyed and left-wing people suppressed too often.

RASKIN: I can remember vaguely the atmosphere of the 1950s. There was mass paranoia, people were afraid to express their ideas. I imagine that you've felt that climate very deeply.

LESSING: In the USA radicals haven't had an easy time. McCarthyism has had a long-term effect on this country and on England, and it hasn't been measured. A great many American friends of mine were destroyed by McCarthy. You told me yesterday that you had seen Morton Sobell and heard him speak. You can't imagine how great a shock it was for me to hear you mention his name casually as you did, because fifteen years ago nobody ever mentioned his name, except for a small circle of radicals. Nobody listened to you if you protested about the treatment of the Rosenbergs and Morton Sobell. Their names made people recoil with horror. In England I helped circulate a petition for the Rosenbergs. It was appallingly hard to get signatures. The atmosphere was violently anti-left; we were on a knife's edge all that time. It's a good thing that young people have escaped that atmosphere. They are freer and braver, but they should realize that McCarthyism can reappear.

RASKIN: It seems to me that your political experience in Africa would be relevant to the experience of white and black radicals today. Could you say something about it?

LESSING: The Communist Party in South Africa was like a seven-year flower which blooms and vanishes. It came into existence in the twenties, but it spread and burgeoned toward the end of the thirties. The Communist Party had an enormous effect on politics because it ignored the colour bar. In the Communist Party white and black people worked together on the basis of equality. Unfortunately, there were more whites than blacks in the party. If there was a Communist Party there today it would have to be predominantly black. But I don't see how blacks can organize anything coherent at the moment. What's likely to happen is sporadic outbreaks of violence by heroic anarchists. Another weakness of the South African Communist Party was its attitude toward the Soviet Union. But it organized trade unions and blacks. When it was banned it went underground and collapsed. Only a handful of brave individuals survived.

RASKIN: The black South African is much more exploited and oppressed than the Afro-American, I imagine.

LESSING: The Africans are fed lies day and night. Every African township has police spies and government informers. A great section of the African population is corrupt, bought off. The black worker, especially the miner, lives in what amounts to a concentration camp. He's policed, doctored, fed, watched. He hasn't got freedom. He's well fed by African standards, but he's a slave. South Africa is a fascist paradise. It's one of the most brilliant police states in history.

RASKIN: Some of the things you've said about radicals and repression remind me of the ending of *The Golden Notebook*, which has puzzled me. Could you explain it?

LESSING: When I wrote *The Golden Notebook* the left was getting one hammer blow after another. Everybody I knew was reeling because the left had collapsed. The scene at the end when Molly goes off and gets married and Anna goes off to do welfare work and joins the Labour Party was intended as a sign of the times. I was being a bit grim about what I observed about me. Women who had been active for years in socialist movements gritted their teeth and said, 'Right, the hell with all this politics, we'll go off and be welfare workers.' They meant it as a kind of joke, but they carried out their programme. They did everything and anything that took them out of politics. Women who had refused to get married because they were dedicated to the cause made marriages which they would have found disgusting five years earlier. They regarded it as a kind of selling out. Brilliant Communist Party organizers went into business and entertainment and became rich men. This didn't happen to everyone, but it happened to many communists.

RASKIN: Many of the New Left students are from Old Left families who are now well off. The sons of famous Establishment professors are in SDS. How do you see the generations?

LESSING: The strain of watching the horrors becomes so great that middle-aged people block them out. My generation doesn't understand that young people have penetrated below the surface and have seen the horrors of our civilization. We've been so damned corrupted. Humanity has gotten worse and worse, puts up with more and more, gets more and more bourgeois. The youth have realized this.

I have always observed incredible brutality in society. My parents' lives and the lives of millions of people were ruined by the First World War. But the human imagination rejects the implications of our situation. War scars humanity in ways we refuse to recognize. After the Second World War the world sat up, licked its wounds ineffectually, and started to prepare for the Third World War. To look at the scene today, to see what man has done to himself, is an incitement to young people to riot. I'm surprised that the New Left isn't more violent.

I hope you don't regard me as unduly bitter. Humanity is a brave lot of people. Everyone of my lot has had to fight on two fronts. Being a Red is tough. My personal experience isn't bad, but friends of mine have been destroyed. The revolutionary movements they were working in sold them down the river. The ex-communists of my lot have lost a certain kind of belief.

RASKIN: What is it you've lost? Isn't it possible that the political struggles of my generation can revive that belief?

LESSING: The ex-communists of my lot can't be surprised by anything. There is no horror that one cannot expect from people. We've learned that.

Well, yours is a new young generation, and with a bit of luck the New Left won't have the kind of hammering my generation did. Maybe it'll be different. Maybe it'll not be the way I think it will be. But you and your generation need a calm to negotiate the rapids.

A Talk with Doris Lessing

BY FLORENCE HOWE

My father, by white terms, was poor . . . But he had 3,000 acres of land. He paid 10 bob an acre for it, and this was land off which Africans had been thrown – into reserves . . . After the Second World War, they did this all again. And for all I know, they're doing it now, this very minute. They 'opened up an area to white occupation,' as they call it, and the whites coming back from the war got it, and I think it cost 5 bob an acre. Maybe it was 10. The white farmer is given a whopping big loan from the land bank, and he's in business. My father employed, depending on the season, anywhere between forty to sixty Africans, and an adult male was paid 12/6 a month, which is what, $1.50? The African is given a day to build himself a hut in the compound. He'll dig a trench, cut some logs, put in the logs, throw some mud on the logs, put some thatch on top of that, and in that he will live. There's no sanitation. A great many farms are like this, as I speak. I'm not talking about vanished conditions.

Since I came to England – I've been here for sixteen years – the whole attitude has changed about colour – in two ways. When I came, South Africa hardly existed except for a tiny group of left wingers who went on about it. Now it's in everybody's consciousness. Nobody ever heard of Rhodesia – it didn't exist. Now there's a kind of political consciousness that is new. And the other thing, very strong, is a colour prejudice in this country – in England – that hasn't begun to really show. I think we're going to be appalled when it shows . . .

Prejudice is very deep in this country, anti-semitism and anti-colour. But you'll find middle-class people with exactly the same prejudices, using careful language but showing it whereas working-class people are likely to come out with it. And I prefer that. I prefer it 'out' to a kind of hidden language, because people these days who will use language to conceal what they really feel are likely to be concealing it from themselves as well, and that is frightening. It's much more frightening than someone in the open, someone who says, 'I'd like to bash those niggers if they take my job,' something straightforward about that.

What about Vietnam?

I can't say anything about Vietnam except a sense of despair, really. Can one really see this ending? Nobody wants to end it fast, except the Vietnamese. I don't know what's the matter with us. What struck me recently is that somewhere buried in me is a foolish idealist that believes that people must be ashamed of behaving badly. Then I read about white people beating up black children and not being ashamed of it. Almost as if there's a permanent boil in the human soul.

Do you find it difficult to write?

Actually I'm too prolific. But I agree with Virginia Woolf that everybody should have a private income – what was it, £500 a year? Five hundred a year would have made all the difference to my life. Even now.

Why do you consider The Golden Notebook *a failure?*

The Golden Notebook was an extremely carefully constructed book. And the way it's constructed says what the book is about – which very few people have understood . . . What *The Golden Notebook* is taken to be by practically everyone is a latter-day feminism. What I was doing is this: I was thinking about the kind of ideas we take for granted . . . a complex of ideas which could be described as left – and which were born with the French Revolution. And they're all to do with freedom. They are revolutionary ideas that are no longer revolutionary and have been absorbed into the fabric of how we live. And they're ideas that fit together in a system, broadly speaking, nonreligious in the old sense, and have to do with the individual in relation to his society and the rights of the individual. Which is a new idea and we don't realize how new it is. We take it absolutely for granted. Three hundred years ago it wouldn't have been taken for granted. And in parts of the world now it wouldn't be – they'd just look at you and not know what you were talking about. But we take it for granted . . .

There was a time in my life when I was a member of a communist group which was pure – they had no contact with any kind of reality. It must have been blessed by Lenin from his grave, it was so pure. The thing was, if we had been in any other part of the world, where in fact there was a Communist Party, the beautiful purity of the ideas that we were trying to operate couldn't have worked. I found this when I came to England and had a short association with the British Communist Party.

Was this in Rhodesia?

Well, the point was there was no Communist Party in Rhodesia. And for a period of about three years, a group of enormously idealistic and mostly extremely intellectual people created a Communist Party in a vacuum which no existing Communist Party anywhere in the world would have recognized as such. But you see, this experience is not so way out as one might think, because if you talk to other communists – communism isn't one thing; it varies from country to country – you find that's what left-wing movements have in common, I think, and this is true not only of the Communist Party, but certainly true of left-wing labour: one is always living in a state of embattled ideas. In fact, *nothing is taken for granted* . . .

I thought that if I wrote a book about the kind of experiences that people I knew had had, I would in fact be writing a book about the kind of ideas people were having – almost as a record. I wrote from inside a woman's viewpoint, naturally, since I am one. Ideas about equality of women and so on. Inside any left-wing group I've been a member of – these ideas are always there, being debated in one way or another and fought out in private relationships. But they are the ideas you would find in the *Sunday Times Supplement* in a cruder form – they're the same ideas. What I'm trying to say is that the left-wing idea is not left wing at all. Because it always has to do with the individual, the rights of. Rights. Fair play. Justice. When *The Golden Notebook* came out, I was astonished that people got so emotional about that book, one way or another. They didn't bother to see, even to look at, how it was shaped. I could mention a dozen books by male authors in which the attitudes to women are the obverse, mirror attitudes, of the attitudes to men in *The Golden Notebook*. But no one would say that these men are anti-women. They would say – I don't know – this man has a problem or he's screwed up, or something. Because after all, deep problems very often are expressed through sex. But I articulated the same things from a female point of view, and this is what was interesting. It was taken as a kind of banner.

In the last generation women have become what is known

as free. And I don't want to get into an argument about how free they are – that's not the point. The point is they're still fighting battles to get free – and rightly. And men are still – some men, you know – some men resist it. But what is interesting, what interests me – what interests me in that book – was, in fact, the ideas. And they still interest me because you have to be apart, a little bit, from an idea before you can see it, even in association with another one. What I'm trying to say is that it was a detached book. It was a failure, of course, for if it had been a success, then people wouldn't get so damned emotional when I didn't want them to be . . .

Women will say to one another in conversation, or to their own private man, something they'd never dream of saying publicly for fear of being called anti-feminine or anti-male. The relationship between the sexes everywhere, not just in Western society, is so much of a melting pot. It's like the colour bar – all kinds of emotions that don't belong get sucked in. You know, I'm convinced that all sorts of emotions that have nothing to do with colour get associated around the colour bar. Similarly with men and women, any sort of loaded point sucks in anger or fear . . . I don't think we understand nearly as much as we think we understand about what goes on.

You know, the *Free Women* section in *The Golden Notebook* – the envelope – I was really trying to express my sense of despair about writing a conventional novel in that. Actually that is an absolutely whole conventional novel, and the rest of the book is the material that went into making it. One of the things I was saying was: Well, look, this is a conventional novel. God knows, I write them myself and doubtless will again. One has this feeling after writing a novel. There it is: 120,000 words; it's got a nice shape and the reviewers will say this and that.

And the bloody complexity that went into it. And it's always a lie. And the terrible despair. So you've written a good novel or a moderate novel, but what does it actually say about what you've actually experienced? The truth is – absolutely nothing. Because you can't. I don't know what one does about novels. I shall write volume 5 [of 'Children of Violence'] with my usual enthusiasm. I know perfectly well that when I've finished it I shall think, Christ, what a lie. Because you can't get life into it – that's all there is to it – no matter how hard you try.

And you think you have in The Golden Notebook, *in the non-novel sections?*

Well, at least I think it's more truthful because it's more complex. People *are* like other people. I mean, I don't think we are as extraordinary as we like to think we are. We are more like other people than we would wish to believe. The same people occur again and again in our lives. Situations do. And any moment of time is so complicated. I like *The Golden Notebook* even though I believe it to be a failure, because it at least hints at complexity.

My Father

We use our parents like recurring dreams, to be entered into when needed; they are always there for love or for hate; but it occurs to me that I was not always there for my father. I've written about him before, but novels, stories, don't have to be 'true.' Writing this article is difficult because it has to be 'true.' I knew him when his best years were over.

There are photographs of him. The largest is of an officer in the 1914-18 war. A new uniform – buttoned, badged, strapped, tabbed – confines a handsome dark young man who holds himself stiffly to confront what he certainly thought of as his duty. His eyes are steady, serious, and responsible, and show no signs of what he became later. A photograph at sixteen is of a dark, introspective youth with the same intent eyes. But it is his mouth you notice – a heavily-jutting upper lip contradicts the rest of a regular face. His moustache was to hide it: 'Had to do something – a damned fleshy mouth. Always made me uncomfortable, that mouth of mine.'

Earlier a baby (eyes already alert) appears in a lace waterfall that cascades from the pillowy bosom of a fat, plain woman to her feet. It is the face of a head cook. 'Lord, but my mother was a practical female – almost as bad as you!' as he used to say, or throw at my mother in moments of exasperation. Beside her stands, or droops, arms dangling, his father, the source of the dark, arresting eyes, but otherwise masked by a long beard.

The birth certificate says: Born 3rd August, 1886, Walton Villa, Creffield Road, S. Mary at the Wall, R.S.D. Name, Alfred Cook. Name and surname of Father: Alfred Cook Tayler. Name and maiden name of Mother: Caroline May Batley. Rank or Profession: Bank Clerk. Colchester, Essex.

They were very poor. Clothes and boots were a problem. They 'made their own amusements.' Books were mostly the Bible and *The Pilgrim's Progress.* Every Saturday night they bathed in a hip-bath in front of the kitchen fire. No servants. Church three times on Sundays. 'Lord, when I think of those Sundays! I dreaded them all week, like a nightmare coming at you full tilt and no escape.' But he rabbited with ferrets along the lanes and fields, bird-nested, stole fruit, picked nuts and mushrooms, paid visits to the blacksmith and the mill and rode a farmer's carthorse.

They ate economically, but when he got diabetes in his forties and subsisted on lean meat and lettuce leaves, he remembered suet puddings, treacle puddings, raisin and currant puddings, steak and kidney puddings, bread and butter pudding, batter cooked in the gravy with the meat, potato cake, plum cake, butter cake, porridge with treacle, fruit tarts and pies, brawn, pig's trotters and pig's cheek and home-smoked ham and sausages. And 'lashings of fresh butter and cream and eggs.' He wondered if this diet had produced the diabetes, but said it was worth it.

There was an elder brother described by my father as: 'Too damned clever by half. One of those quick, clever brains. Now I've always had a slow brain, but I get there in the end, damn it!'

The brothers went to a local school and the elder did well, but my father was beaten for being slow. They both became bank clerks in, I think, the Westminster Bank, and one must have found it congenial, for he became a manager, the 'rich brother,' who had cars and even a yacht. But my father did not like it, though he was conscientious. For instance, he changed his writing, letter by letter, because a senior criticized it. I never saw his unregenerate hand, but the one he created was elegant, spiky, careful. Did this mean he created a new personality for himself, hiding one he did not like, as he hid his 'damned fleshy mouth'? I don't know.

Nor do I know when he left home to live in Luton or why. He found family life too narrow? A safe guess – he found everything too narrow. His mother was too down-to-earth? He had to get away from his clever elder brother ?

Being a young man in Luton was the best part of his life. It ended in 1914, so he had a decade of happiness. His reminiscences of it were all of pleasure, the delight of physical movement, of dancing in particular. All his girls were 'a beautiful dancer, light as a feather.' He played billiards and ping-pong (both for his county); he swam, boated, played cricket and football, went to picnics and horse races, sang at musical evenings. One family of a mother and two daughters treated him 'like a son only better. I didn't know whether I was in love with the mother or the daughters, but oh I did love going there; we had such good times.' He was engaged to one daughter, then, for a time, to the other. An engagement was broken off because she was rude to a waiter. 'I could not marry a woman who allowed herself to insult someone who was defenceless.' He used to say to my wryly smiling mother: 'Just as well I didn't marry either of *them*; they would never have stuck it out the way you have, old girl.'

Just before he died he told me he had dreamed he was standing in a kitchen on a very high mountain holding X in his arms. 'Ah, yes, that's what I've missed in my life. Now don't you let yourself be cheated out of life by the old dears. They take all the colour out of everything if you let them.'

But in that decade – 'I'd walk 10, 15 miles to a dance two or three times a week and think nothing of it. Then I'd dance every dance and walk home again over the fields. Sometimes it was moonlight, but I liked the snow best, all crisp and fresh. I loved walking back and getting into my digs just as the sun was rising. My little dog was so happy to see me, and I'd feed her, and make myself porridge and tea, then I'd wash and shave and go off to work.'

The boy who was beaten at school, who went too much to church, who carried the fear of poverty all his life, but who nevertheless was filled with the memories of country pleasures; the young bank clerk who worked such long hours for so little money, but who danced, sang, played, flirted – this naturally vigorous, sensuous being was killed in 1914, 1915, 1916. I think the best of my father died in that war, that his spirit was crippled by it. The people I've met, particularly the women, who knew him young, speak of his high spirits, his energy, his enjoyment of life. Also of his kindness, his compassion and – a word that keeps recurring – his wisdom. 'Even when he was just a boy he understood things that you'd think even an old man would find it easy to condemn.' I do not think these people would have easily recognized the ill, irritable abstracted, hypochondriac man I knew.

He 'joined up' as an ordinary soldier out of a character-istically quirky scruple: it wasn't right to enjoy officers' privi-leges when the Tommies had such a bad time. But he could not stick the communal latrines, the obligatory drinking, the col-lective visits to brothels, the jokes about girls. So next time he was offered a commission he took it.

His childhood and young man's memories, kept fluid, were added to, grew, as living memories do. But his war memories were congealed in stories that he told again and again, with the same words and gestures, in stereotyped phrases. They were anonymous, general, as if they had come out of a com-munal war memoir. He met a German in no-man's-land, but both slowly lowered thar rifles and smiled and walked away.

The Tommies were the salt of the earth, the British fighting men the best in the world. He had never known such comradeship. A certain brutal officer was shot in a sortie by his men, but the other officers, recognizing rough justice, said nothing. He had known men intimately who saw the Angels at Mons. He wished he could force all the generals on both sides into the trenches for just one day, to see what the common soldiers endured – *that* would have ended the war at once.

There was an undercurrent of memories, dreams, and emotions much deeper, more personal. This dark region in him, fate-ruled, where nothing was true but horror, was expressed inarticulately, in brief, bitter exclamations or phrases of rage, incredulity, betrayal. The men who went to fight in that war believed it when they said it was to end war. My father believed it. And he was never able to reconcile his belief in his country with his anger at the cynicism of its leaders. And the anger, the sense of betrayal, strengthened as he grew old and ill.

But in 1914 he was naïve, the German atrocities in Belgium inflamed him, and he enlisted out of idealism, although he knew he would have a hard time. He knew because a fortune-teller told him. (He could be described as uncritically superstitious or as psychically gifted.) He would be in great danger twice, yet not die – he was being protected by a famous soldier who was his ancestor. 'And sure enough, later I heard from the Little Aunties that the church records showed we were descended the backstairs way from the Duke of Wellington, or was it Marlborough? Damn it, I forget. But one of them would be beside me all through the war, she said.' (He was romantic, not only about this solicitous ghost, but also about being a descendant of the Huguenots, on the strength of the 'e' in Tayler; and about 'the wild blood' in his veins from a great uncle who, sent unjustly to prison for smuggling, came out of a ten-year sentence and earned it, very efficiently, along the coasts of Cornwall until he died.)

The luckiest thing that ever happened to my father, he said, was getting his leg shattered by shrapnel ten days before Passchendaele. His whole company was killed. He knew he was going to be wounded because of the fortune-teller, who had said he would know. 'I did not understand what she meant, but both times in the trenches, first when my appendix burst and I nearly died, and then just before Passchendaele, I felt for some days as if a thick, black velvet pall was settled over me. I can't tell you what it was like. Oh, it was awful, awful, and the second time it was so bad I wrote to the old people and told them I was going to be killed.'

His leg was cut off at mid-thigh, he was shell-shocked, he was very ill for many months, with a prolonged depression afterwards. 'You should always remember that sometimes people are all seething underneath. You don't know what terrible things people have to fight against. You should look at a person's eyes, that's how you tell . . . When I was like that, after I lost my leg, I went to a nice doctor man and said I was going mad, but he said, don't worry, everyone locks up things like that. You don't know – horrible, horrible, awful things. I was afraid of myself, of what I used to dream. I wasn't myself at all.'

In the Royal Free Hospital was my mother, Sister McVeagh. He married his nurse which, as they both said often enough (though in different tones of voice), was just as well. That was 1919. He could not face being a bank clerk in England, he said, not after the trenches. Besides, England was too narrow and conventional. Besides, the civilians did not know what the soldiers had suffered, they didn't want to know, and now it wasn't done even to remember 'The Great Unmentionable.' He went off to the Imperial Bank of Persia, in which country I was born.

The house was beautiful, with great stone-floored high-ceilinged rooms whose windows showed ranges of snow-streaked mountains. The gardens were full of roses, jasmine, pomegranates, walnuts. Kermanshah he spoke of with liking, but soon they went to Tehran, populous with 'Embassy people,' and my gregarious mother created a lively social life about which he was irritable even in recollection.

Irritableness – that note was first struck here, about Persia. He did not like, he said, 'the graft and the corruption.' But here it is time to try and describe something difficult – how a man's good qualities can also be his bad ones, or if not bad, a danger to him.

My father was honourable – he always knew exactly what that word meant. He had integrity. His 'one does not do that sort of thing,' his 'no, it is *not* right,' sounded throughout my childhood and were final for all of us. I am sure it was true he wanted to leave Persia because of 'the corruption.' But it was also because he was already unconsciously longing for something freer, because as a bank official he could not let go into the dream-logged personality that was waiting for him. And later in Rhodesia, too, what was best in him was also what prevented him from shaking away the shadows: it was always in the name of honesty or decency that he refused to take this step or that out of the slow decay of the family's fortunes.

In 1925 there was leave from Persia. That year in London there was an Empire Exhibition, and on the Southern Rhodesian stand some very fine maize cobs and a poster saying that fortunes could be made on maize at 25/- a bag. So on an impulse, turning his back forever on England, washing his hands of the corruption of the East, my father collected all his capital, £800, I think, while my mother packed curtains from Liberty's, clothes from Harrods, visiting cards, a piano, Persian rugs, a governess and two small children.

Soon, there was my father in a cigar-shaped house of thatch

and mud on the top of a kopje that overlooked in all directions a great system of mountains, rivers, valleys, while overhead the sky arched from horizon to empty horizon. This was a couple of hundred miles south from the Zambesi, a hundred or so west from Mozambique in the district of Banket, so called because certain of its reefs were of the same formation as those called *banket* on the Rand. Lomagundi – gold country, tobacco country, maize country – wild, almost empty, (The Africans had been turned off it into reserves.) Our neighbours were four, five, seven miles off. In front of the house . . . no neighbours, nothing; no farms, just wild bush with two rivers but no fences to the mountains seven miles away. And beyond these mountains and bush again to the Portuguese border, over which 'our boys' used to escape when wanted by the police for pass or other offences.

And then? There was bad luck. For instance, the price of maize dropped from 25/- to 9/- a bag. The seasons were bad, prices bad, crops failed. This was the sort of thing that made it impossible for him ever to 'get off the farm,' which, he agreed with my mother, was what he most wanted to do. It was an absurd country, he said. A man could 'own' a farm for years that was totally mortgaged to the Government and run from the Land Bank, meanwhile employing half-a-hundred Africans at 12/- a month and none of them knew how to do a day's work. Why, two farm labourers from Europe could do in a day what twenty of these ignorant black savages would take a week to do. (Yet he was proud that he had a name as a just employer, that he gave 'a square deal.') Things got worse. A fortune-teller had told him that her heart ached when she saw the misery ahead for my father: this was the misery.

But it was my mother who suffered. After a period of neurotic illness, which was a protest against her situation, she became brave and resourceful. But she never saw that her husband was not living in a real world, that he had made a captive of her common sense. We were always about to 'get off the farm.' A miracle would do it – a sweepstake, a goldmine, a legacy. And then? What a question! We would go to England where life would be normal with people coming in for musical evenings and nice supper parties at the Trocadero after a show. Poor woman, for the twenty years we were on the farm, she waited for when life would begin for her and for her children, for she never understood that what was a calamity for her was for them a blessing.

Meanwhile my father sank towards his death (at 61). Everything changed in him. He had been a dandy and fastidious, now he hated to change out of shabby khaki. He had been sociable, now he was misanthropic. His body's disorders – soon diabetes and all kinds of stomach ailments – dominated him. He was brave about his wooden leg, and even went down mine shafts and climbed trees with it, but he walked clumsily and it irked him badly. He greyed fast, and slept more in the day, but would be awake half the night pondering about . . .

It could be gold divining. For ten years he experimented on private theories to do with the attractions and repulsions of metals. His whole soul went into it but his theories were wrong or he was *unlucky* – after all, if he had found a mine he would have had to leave the farm. It could be the relation between the minerals of the earth and of the moon; his decision to make infusions of all the plants on the farm and drink them himself in the interests of science; the criminal folly of the British Government in not realizing that the Germans and the Russians were conspiring as Anti-Christ to . . . the inevitability of war because no one would listen to Churchill, but it would be all right because God (by then he was a British Israelite) had destined Britain to rule the world; a prophecy said 10 million dead would surround Jerusalem – how would the corpses be cleared away?; people who wished to abolish flogging should be flogged; the natives understood nothing but a good beating; hanging must not be abolished because the Old Testament said 'an eye for an eye and a tooth for a tooth . . .'

Yet, as this side of him darkened, so that it seemed all his thoughts were of violence, illness, war, still no one dared to make an unkind comment in his presence or to gossip. Criticism of people, particularly of women, made him more and more uncomfortable till at last he burst out with: 'It's all very well, but no one has the right to say that about another person.'

In Africa, when the sun goes down, the stars spring up, all of them in their expected places, glittering and moving. In the rainy season, the sky flashed and thundered. In the dry season, the great dark hollow of night was lit by veld fires: the mountains burned through September and October in chains of red fire. Every night my father took out his chair to watch the sky and the mountains, smoking, silent, a thin shabby fly-away figure under the stars. 'Makes you think – there are so many worlds up there, wouldn't really matter if we did blow ourselves up – plenty more where we came from.'

The Second World War, so long foreseen by him, was a bad time. His son was in the Navy and in danger, and his daughter a sorrow to him. He became very ill. More and more often it was necessary to drive him into Salisbury with him in a coma, or in danger of one, on the back seat. My mother moved him into a pretty little suburban house in town near the hospitals, where he took to his bed and a couple of years later died. For the most part he was unconscious under drugs. When awake he talked obsessively (a tongue licking a nagging sore place) about 'the old war.' Or he remembered his youth. 'I've been dreaming – Lord, to see those horses come lickety-split down the course with their necks stretched out and the sun on their coats and everyone shouting . . . I've been dreaming how I

walked along the river in the mist as the sun was rising . . .
Lord, lord, lord, what a time that was, what good times we all
had then, before the old war.'

Impertinent Daughters

I

A photograph of my mother shows her as a large, round-faced schoolgirl, full of the confidence I have to associate with her being Victorian. Her hair is tied back with a black bow. She is wearing her school uniform, a full white blouse and a long dark skirt. In a photograph taken forty-five years later, she appears as a lean, severe old thing, bravely looking out from a world of disappointment and frustration. She stands by my father, her hand on the back of his chair. He has to sit: as always, he is ill. It is clear that he is only just holding himself together, but he is in a proper suit, certainly because she has told him he must make the effort. She wears a rather smart tailored dress, made up out of a remnant bought in the sales.

The difference between these photographs is what this memoir has to be about. It seems that it has taken me a lifetime to understand my parents, with astonishments all the way. There is a mysterious process, frightening because there is nothing whatsoever you can do about it, that takes you from fierce adolescence – as if parents and you stood at either side of a battlefield, hands full of weapons – to a place where you can stand where they did, in imagination, any time you want.

Only when I sat down to write this did it occur to me that I could write about my father and hardly mention that dread word 'class,' but with my mother it is a different matter. She never freed her judgements from thoughts of class, but then she did not see why she should. Class was then a straitjacket, an imperative, a crippler. Only that time, that place, could have produced her: London, Britain, the British Empire. But the Empire was in its last days: a thought she would have dismissed as treacherous, wrongheaded, soft.

On a mud wall of the old house on the farm in Africa where I was brought up was a large, ornately framed portrait of my grandfather McVeagh. He is standing beside his second wife. He was fat-faced and overfed, with hair slicked down on either side of a parting. He wore a tight smug suit, and a golden chain across his chest. I loathed him, this self-righteous prig, with a violence that stopped me from listening to my mother, whose reminiscences seemed only another attempt to bind me to her. Had she, had my father, not escaped from England? Why, then, was she winding me back into that shroud? I closed my ears, and I am sorry now I did. For instance, who was that elegant, fastidious lady he married? She was Jewish*, with a fine curved nose and exquisite hands. Her dress was a miracle of embroidery and little tucks and lace. She came from a different world, by nature if not by class. I think she was a governess. Yet she had chosen to marry him: a thought that didn't enter my head for years, he made two romantic marriages, this philistine bank manager.

Once I had a fit of wanting to know who my forebears were, and before I found what a fussy and tedious business it is and gave it up, I came across birth certificates of McVeaghs from Exeter and Maidstone. They were all called John and Edward and James, and were sergeants in cavalry regiments. In short, my grandfather McVeagh, or his father,

* At the original time of writing, I was under the impression she was Jewish. I was mistaken.

had made the jump up into the middle classes, and he was as snobbish as one would expect. Yet his first marriage had been to Emily Flower, the daughter of a contractor for lightering. A marriage for love. There is no picture of Emily Flower. This is because she was such a misfortune. All my childhood I heard of this grandmother thus: 'She was very pretty, but all she cared about was dancing and horses.' It was said with the little cold sniff that probably derived from the servants who brought the children up after wicked Emily died, which was – my mother's tone said it served her right – in childbirth with her third child. That was in 1888, and she was thirty-two. But how was it that the wife of a suburban bank manager was able to dance all the time and be mad about horses? In Blackheath? Blackheath was where my mother said the tall, grim, cold house was; but on Emily's death certificate it says Canning Town.

My mother, Emily Maude, was the first child. Then came Uncle John. Then Muriel, who disgraced herself and the family by marrying back into the working class. Hardly a surprise, judged my mother, for Muriel was always happiest with the servants. In other words she was not happy in the competitive, striving atmosphere of getting on and doing well.

It was a cold home. Her father, so romantic in love, ruled his children as Victorian papas are reputed to have done, with the rod, and without love. There was no affection from the elegant stepmother, who was dutiful and correct and did not understand children. I never once heard my mother speak of her father with warmth. Respect, yes; prescribed admiration, certainly. Never love. As for her stepmother, she might have been a visitor or a distant relation.

Emily was clever at school, much cleverer than her brother, John, who was destined for the Navy, and who found the exams difficult. He had to be coached and pushed and prodded. She loved examinations, came first in class, adored mathematics, and was expected for a time to become a professional pianist.

The children, as was proper in this Forsytian world, were taken to all public occasions of rejoicing or grief; and my mother spoke of Mafeking night, Queen Victoria's funeral, the coronation of Edward VII, exhibitions, the visits of the Kaiser and of foreign heads of government, as if these milestones were the only possible way to mark the passing of a childhood.

If there was little family life, there was an energetic social life full of friends she kept in touch with for years, even from the farm in Africa. She played tennis and lacrosse and hockey and went on bicycle trips. There were musical evenings. They drew portraits of each other and pictures of appropriate landscapes; wrote humorous and sentimental verses to mark anniversaries. They pressed flowers and collected shells, birds' eggs and stones. They visited the theatre with suppers afterwards at the Trocadero. All this went on in London: she was essentially urban, this woman who would find herself on a farm in the veld.

Modern-minded John William McVeagh, proud of his clever daughter, was thinking of university for her, but was confronted with a rebellious girl who said she wanted to be a nurse. He was horrified, utterly overthrown. Middle-class girls did not become nurses, and he didn't want to hear anything about Florence Nightingale. Any skivvy could be a nurse, and if you become one, do not darken my door! Very well, said Emily Maude, and went off to the old Royal Free Hospital to begin her training. It was hard: conditions were bad, the pay was low, but she did well, and when she brilliantly passed her finals, her father was prepared to forgive her. She never forgave him. She had done it all on her own, without him.

Whom, then, did she love, this poor girl brought up without affection? She was fond of her brother, John, but this was a far from simple emotion, and of course he was at boarding school most of the time. Her sister, Muriel, was not her sort. Her many and varied friends? They were good sports, pals . . . Why did she fight so hard to become a nurse, if not that she needed to care for and to nurture people and to be loved for it? I have only just had this thought: I could have had it before.

Her training completed, she resumed, as far as possible, her social life. She had given up dreams of being a pianist, but continued to play the organ for churches, for instance, in Langham Place. She was part, in a small way, of the musical life of London. 'I could have been a real concert pianist,' she would say, until the end of her days. 'I had my LRAM [Licentiate of the Royal Academy of Music]. The Examiners told me I should go on.' I wonder at her energy. Nurses worked harder then than now. Yet there were musical evenings, and concerts, and excursions. Also, holidays – always sea trips, for she loved the sea. She read, too, as did my father. Both knew enough of Wells and Shaw to be affected, and both judged society from a perspective of critical independence. There was a generation of young people, before the First World War, for whom Wells and Shaw played the same tutoring role as Orwell did later.

Then began the War. 1914. She was a sister in the Royal Free Hospital, nursing the wounded soldiers who arrived in trainloads from the trenches. She had an album with verses written by the men she nursed back to life, and she appears as the traditional martinet with a heart of gold.

My father, at that time, was fighting in the trenches. He had two periods there. The first was ended by a timely appendix, otherwise he would have been killed with all his company in the Battle of the Somme. The second, timely again, was when he was wounded – shrapnel in the leg – preventing him from being killed with every other man in the company, at Passchendaele. I do not know exactly how long he was in the trenches, but altogether it was months. He said he was lucky not to have been killed a dozen times over. But the war did him in nevertheless: he lost his leg, and was psychologically damaged. He went into the fighting active and optimistic, and came out with what they then called shell shock. He was in bed for months. My mother nursed him. He was very ill, she said, and what was so worrying was his state of mind. I have a photograph of him in bed in the Royal Free Hospital, a handsome man, but minus a leg and inwardly in torment. Beside him Sister McVeagh sits wearing her full white veil, sewing, her eyes on her handiwork. 'Before she was thought of,' says the caption, meaning me, their first child. The date is September 1917.

She was thirty-three, a year older than her mother had been when she died giving birth to her third child. Sister McVeagh was facing a hard, a very hard, choice. She had been asked if she would accept the matronship of St George's Hospital – an honour, at her age. Usually much older women became matrons and ran great hospitals. But she liked nursing: did she want to become an administrator? Besides, matrons were such martinets! She had suffered under these formidable women, did she want to become one? And here was Captain Tayler, of whom she had become very fond, wanting to marry her. There were no men left, they were all killed. Would she be asked again? She had always thought of herself as – had always been told she was – very plain. Did she want to marry him? Did she want to marry at all, since her real love, the man she ought to have married, was dead?

He had been a young doctor in the hospital with whom, my father confirmed, she had had an understanding. His little picture, torn out of a newspaper that recorded his death by drowning in a ship sunk by the Germans, stood forever on her dressing table. He had a soft, boyish face. The understanding between them, the death, my mother's unhappiness were observed by my father, who always spoke of him with pain. 'Your poor mother,' he would say, 'he was a good chap, that young doctor.'

It took her a long time to decide, and she became ill with the strain of it all. As a nurse she should have known what she had to face in a man so damaged. Later she would say, often: 'If we knew when we were young what was going to happen to us, then . . .'

She really had no idea, then or ever, of the mental world my father lived in. I am not only talking of his depression after the war. Quite simply, he had a dimension that she lacked. For a long time I thought it was the awfulness of the war that had given him his sensitiveness to other people, his broadness of outlook. Their experiences, after all, had not been so different. His upbringing had been as bad as hers – savage, I was going to say, and yes, the word can stand: her impatient ruthlessness, I once thought, was the legacy of her childhood. But he had been much beaten at school and at home, over-disciplined, and harshly misunderstood. He, like her, had escaped as soon as he could. Years later I met people who had known him as a young man – and what the war had done was to confirm his essential nature: he had always been contemplative and philosophical. 'Your father had his own way of seeing things,' cried a former girlfriend, 'and I would often rather not have known what he was thinking.' And another said, not without ambiguity, that she had never been so well understood. He was kind; he was generous; she had not met anyone like him; but there was something detached in him which was hard to take. And this detachment was a part of his deepest characteristic – an understanding of impermanence, change.

I believe that his nature, so different from hers, was why my mother married him. She knew she had limitations – how could she not, brought up constantly against this magnanimity in everything? 'Don't you see, old girl, that's how things *are*?' he would say, amazed at her pettiness, her inability to see: he had been watching Life at it again, working out one of its little games. He was unsurprised, interested: she, always, rebellious.

To put her dilemma squarely: what she respected most in him, what gave her access to a largeness she would never have known without him, was precisely what did both her and him in: these fine ways of thinking, his scope, were always overthrowing her best self, which was a magnificent commonsense. She had married a weak man, then? But his weakness was obviously stronger than her strength, always pulling her further away from what would best suit her. A *weak* man? Yet he was not weak by nature; it was the war that had distorted him. Weak! How else could you describe him? Always refusing to make judgements, take stands; always insisting on what he called the long view – you'd think there was nothing he respected . . . And yet. Life was not a simple business; she suspected he was nearer to understanding it than she would ever be.

I have an image of them, confronting Life in such different ways. He looks it straight in the face, with a dark, grim, ironical recognition. But she, always being disappointed in ways he could never be, has a defiant, angry little air: she has caught Life out in injustice again. 'How can you!' she seems to be saying, exasperated, to Life. 'It's not right to behave like that!' And she gives a brisk, brave little sniff.

They were married. They did not feel up to a proper

wedding. For one thing they were Wells and Shaw people, and white weddings were ridiculous (obviously soon to become obsolete!), and for another, his mother disapproved of Sister McVeagh: she was going to rule him with a rod of iron, said this ruler with the rod. My father was elegant, as always, when he still cared about clothes. My mother wore a dress she clearly had given a lot of thought to: only recently, when I was writing the Jane Somers books, did I realize that my mother (who could, I think, be something like Jane Somers if she lived now) very much enjoyed clothes, even though for most of her life she did not have the money to buy them, or the opportunity to wear them.

It was on the wedding night, they joked, that my mother must have got pregnant, though they were armed with the works of Marie Stopes, and had decided not to have a baby yet, if at all. He was still so low in spirits: he simply did not seem able to pull himself out of his ugly state of mind. And she was ill, she did not know why, but it was probably overwork from the war. And there was all that flu about, so many people dying everywhere: everything was so depressing after the war. It was 1919.

They left for Persia. He had to leave England – he couldn't stand it – so why not Persia? My mother, being a woman of her time, was ready to go off and live in the Middle East, even though she knew nothing about it. A close friend was a missionary in Japan; her brother, John, never at home in the Army – he did not pass the Navy exams – was about to become a rubber planter in Malaya.

Persia was then divided into spheres of influence, mainly French and British. Britain had finance, and my father was going to manage a bank in Kermanshah. Before the war he had been a clerk in a bank, and to have to go back to it was awful for him; but at least he was getting out of England, where he knew he could never live again. Coming back from the trenches he felt as all the soldiers of that war did: betrayed by the politicians who had lied to them and did not keep promises; betrayed by the civilians who talked patriotic nonsense and had no idea of what the trenches were like; betrayed by the jingoistic newspapers; betrayed by the Armistice which would make another war inevitable. It was stupid to treat the Germans like this, one should take the long view. None of the Tommies felt vindictive. Any Tommy could tell the politicians they were being stupid. A funny thing, wasn't it? he would demand all his life (my mother half agreeing with him, feeling that she should, while her nature rebelled): any ordinary person could see it, the politicians couldn't. Why is it that ordinary people have so much more sense than politicians when it is the politicians' job to be sensible?

This was the first time in her life when my mother would need a lot of clothes, and she took trunks full of them. She also took the necessities for a middle-class nursery as prescribed by one Dr Truby King and other mentors. The layette for a baby then consisted of dozens of everything. Napkins thick and thin, and napkin liners. Vests long and short, inner and outer. Petticoats of various lengths, of flannel and of lawn, embroidered and tucked and edged with lace. Long and short dresses of pin-tucked and embroidered lawn. Caps. Shawls. Not to mention binders made of thick material which supported the baby's stomach as if it were a wound from which entrails might spill. This layette itself must have been enough to dismay any woman, make her feel helpless, feel at least that an ordeal lay ahead. It all assumed servants of course. Those exquisite dresses alone took hours to iron, not to mention the dressing and undressing of the helpless infant, who was also supposed to be fed every two or three hours day and night, and, if bottle-fed – a recommended practice – the preparations were like those for a surgical operation.

I used to read those lists on the farm in Rhodesia, dazzled by incredulity: I was surrounded by black babies living contented and naked inside a fold of cloth on their mother's backs.

It was 'Maude' and 'Michael' Tayler who arrived in Persia. My mother had always disliked Emily, I suppose because it was the name of her mother, but she liked Maude, because of Tennyson's Maud. She had been trying to shed Emily for years. She would not have Alfred for my father: a common name. And what did he think about it? I can hear him: 'Oh Lord, old thing, who cares? What does it matter? If it makes you happy, then . . .' He was made Michael because of Peter Pan.

The Westminster Bank allotted Maude and Michael an enormous house made of stone that was carved and fretted, with great arches along the verandahs and arched windows, and surrounded by wonderful gardens. Servants – gardeners, cooks, people who cleaned the house, shopped – did everything. My mother hardly mentioned the servants, except to say that households were regulated by protocol, and that the mistress of the house knew her place and did what she was told. She thought this amusing: not a hint here of what in Africa became a neurotic preoccupation – the shortcomings of the black servants.

For my father Kermanshah was what he had dreamed of: an ancient town on a high empty brown landscape, the high blue sky, the mountains all around with the snow on them. When I went to Granada for the first time I knew it was like Kermanshah: gardens, the sounds of water running everywhere, the smell of the dust . . . My father was managing the bank; he was not at anybody's beck and call.

He rode everywhere, for he would not allow his wooden leg to make him less active. He liked the spacious house and the release, at least to an extent, from English respectability.

My mother was having a difficult pregnancy, morning sickness being only one of the complications. She was expecting a son, Peter John. Why did she not even consider the possibility of a daughter? Her passionate identification with a son was, I think, because of her brother, John, who was not clever, did not care very much what he did, and yet went, was expected to go as if by right, into the Navy. I think she most bitterly envied him, but to feel like this was not being a good sort. She was the one born to be an officer in His Majesty's Navy! She was the clever one, who adored everything about the sea, about ships, was never seasick. She was resourceful and quick-witted. She was decent and good-humoured and able to get on with people. An authoritarian personality, happy in a structured life, she was able to take and to give orders. Of course, the negative aspects of this particular personality were also hers: the inability to put herself into the shoes of people who were different; a contempt for weakness; a lack of understanding of what she described as 'morbid': the ambiguous, the witty, the equivocal – these areas would always be suspect, and she was threatened by them.

I can only guess, hurt for her, at how much she must have felt frustrated as a girl, seeing her slow brother expected to get what ought to have been hers too. And yet she never said anything, except in jolly little jokes, brave jokes. What she felt had to come out indirectly.

The birth was difficult. I was delivered with forceps that left a scarlet birthmark over one side of my face. Above all, I was a girl. When the doctor wanted to know my name, and heard that none had been prepared, he looked down at the cradle and said softly, 'Doris?' This scene: the doctor's weariness after the long night, his soft, tactful, but reproach-ful query, was vividly enacted by my mother, like many other scenes.

Of course I resented it all bitterly, particularly that she did not even see that it was likely to make me angry. How could she stand there, with her customary determined little smile, her brisk social manner, telling me that I was not wanted in the first place; that to have a girl was a disappointment that nearly did her in altogether, after that long labour; that she had no milk for me and I had to be bottle-fed from the start and I was half-starved for the first year and never stopped screaming because she did not realize that cows' milk in Persia was not as rich as real English milk; that I was an impossibly difficult baby, and then a tiresome child, quite unlike my little brother, Harry, who was always so good. And so she let the nurse cope with me, and looked after Harry herself.

Better say, and be done with it: my memories of her are all of antagonism, and fighting, and feeling shut out; of pain because the baby born two-and-a-half years after me was so much loved when I was not. She would recognize none of this, nor accept it. The way she saw it was that her childhood had been cold and loveless, and she would make sure that her children were governed by love. Love was always being invoked; and I became an expert in emotional blackmail by the time I was five. She didn't like me – that was the point. It was not her fault: I cannot think of a person less likely than myself to please her. But it would have been impossible for her to admit it: a mother loves her child, a child its mother. And that's that!

My father hated it when he was transferred to Tehran, to a branch of the bank where he was not manager and had to work under someone else, and where he had to live in a house he thought English and stuffy. But my mother loved it. At last, suitable nurseries, instead of those great stone rooms that curtains and rugs could not soften. I remember the tall, square day-nursery, the heavy red velvet curtains and the lace ones behind them, the brass fender with the tall dangerous fire, the suffocating plenty of things, things, things. And, of course, my brother, the 'baby' (he was called Baby until he was seven and fought for self-determination) who was the centre of everything. And the scolding, fussy nurse.

In Tehran my mother also loved the social life, which was like the pleasures of her girlhood over again. About 'the Legation set' she would talk wistfully in Africa, while my father, half sighing, regarded her with his familiar expression: incredulity, curiosity, held in check by irony. How could she enjoy those boring jolly evenings with boring jolly people? He loathed musical evenings, with people singing the 'Indian Love Lyrics' and 'The Road to Mandalay' to each other, while my mother played. (She played alone, for her own pleasure, music these people found highbrow.) He hated the dinner parties, receptions, garden parties, and picnics; she could not have enough of them. He would tell the story of a certain Englishman in Persia who, urged by his family to let them have a picnic, put his children on donkeys, blindfolded them, and had them led around and around the garden for an hour, when they were unblindfolded and saw the feast prepared for them in a corner of their own garden. Meanwhile he retired to the library. A fellow spirit! My mother only laughed. 'Don't you dare try it,' she said.

Persia, particularly Tehran, was the best time in my mother's life.

When they had been in Persia for five years, leave was due, after which they intended to come back. He did not much want to: would he really have to work in a bank for the rest of his life? He had had a country childhood, and always wanted to be a farmer.

114

It was summer, the Red Sea a furnace, and dangerous for children. They decided – which means, my mother decided – to travel back across Russia. Ours was the first family to use that route after the Revolution, through the Caspian to Moscow. 1924, and everything was in chaos. On an oil tanker in the Caspian, my mother sat up all night to keep the lights on us, for there were swarms of lice. A shadow fell on an arm: mine, which became red and swollen with bites. Typhus abounded. The trains were ancient, also lice-ridden, no food on them. On every station were crowds of starved children, orphans; and the peasant women selling a hard-boiled egg or some bread had to defend themselves against these *besprizorniks*, when my mother got off to buy something, anything at all, to eat. She was still on the platform once when our train left without her. I remember the terror of it: she had vanished. It took her a day and a half to catch up. She had to fight her way onto a goods train, had to 'tell them what to do – *they* didn't know – I had to make them telegraph our train to wait for me.' All in English, of course. At the frontier, informed that we did not have the right visas, she had told the man at Immigration not to be so silly. For years my father collapsed into laughter, remembering the poor ragged half-starved Bolshevik with a rifle 'that wouldn't bring down a pigeon,' confronted by a British matron. 'Oh Lord,' wept my father, 'I can see it now. Don't be silly, she said, and he was raring to shoot the lot of us.' 'Did I get us in or did I not?' demanded my mother, not really understanding why he laughed so much, but knowing she was in the right. 'Oh, you got us in all right!'

In Moscow, in the hotel, the chambermaids begged to bath and dress us, because they had not seen normal well-fed children. My mother spoke of this with calm, proprietary pride: that the Russians were in this terrible disorganized condition was of course only another proof of the virtues of the British and our Empire.

Six months' leave, in England. My memories of it are many, all of cold, damp, dreariness, ugliness, a series of snapshots illustrating my loathing for the place. My parents took us to visit relations, such as my mother's stepmother, now a distinguished old lady living on a minute pension. They did not enjoy it. My father wanted only to leave England, even more stuffy than he remembered, and my mother yearned to return to Tehran. They visited the 1924 Empire Exhibition at Wembley, and the Southern Rhodesia stand had maize cobs eighteen inches long, and the posters, yards high, claimed that anyone could make his fortune in maize-farming within five years.

My father had about £1,000 capital and a pension because he had lost his leg in the War. This was his chance.

What did they imagine they were going to? Certainly they expected a social life not unlike that in Tehran, for my mother had trunks full of clothes from Harrods. Also curtains and hangings from Liberty's, and visiting cards. Also a governess, Biddy O'Halloran, aged twenty-one. Perhaps they had heard of the lively goings-on in Nairobi? Not that my mother would have approved of those fast ways. She could not approve of Biddy, who had shingled hair and wore lipstick. These modern girls . . . all her life my mother would use phrases like this, without inverted commas.

It must have been painful, giving up Tehran, to go off to be a farmer's wife in yet another new country. She would not really have minded staying in England – that is to say, London. She was still, every fibre of her, a Londoner. Remembering England, she thought of the streets, buses,

116

trams, theatres, parks, of London. She did not mind the conventional in the way my father did. If he had been prepared to go back into the Westminster Bank somewhere in London, she would have given up the pleasures of Tehran with equanimity. And then she would have lived out her life in conformity with her nature, a useful and energetic middle-class woman in, let's say, Wimbledon.

Instead, she set off for the middle of Africa with her crippled husband, who was steadily getting more prickly and solitary, with practically no money, and her two children, one of whom was born to be a trouble and a sorrow to her. Did she know anything about Africa, or about farming? Not a thing! But it didn't seem to matter.

I think she saw Africa as some little interlude, a station on her way, soon to be passed. Nothing had ever happened to my mother to prepare her for what she would find.

It was a slow German boat. My mother loved the gales that sent the other passengers below, leaving her on the bridge with the captain. This, and the deck games and the fancy-dress parties, made up for her husband, who wanted only to sit and watch the sea, and for her daughter, who was being consistently impertinent, and who cut up her evening dresses with scissors when she was forced to go to bed early so as not to interfere with the evening's good times. The boat loafed around the Cape to Beira, where they caught the train to Salisbury. Outside Salisbury was a place called Lilfordia that boarded settlers while they were buying farms. (Lilfordia was the farm of 'Boss' Lilford, later Ian Smith's guide and mentor.) My mother left her children with the governess, and went with her husband by Scotch cart to look at farms. The settlers were being offered land at about twenty pounds an acre (at today's values), the money advanced by the Land Bank. The land had been cleared of the black people who had been living on it: they were despatched to the Reserves, or told to move to land that hadn't yet been allocated to whites. This was 'opening up the country for white civilization,' a description my mother never could see any reason to criticize.

The farm they bought was in Lomagundi, seventy miles from Salisbury, a modest 1,500 acres, but we were free to run our cattle, and to cut grass and wood on the miles of Government land which remained unallocated all the time we were there. Our farm, then, was at the frontier of 'white civilization' with nothing between us and Portuguese East Africa a couple of hundred miles away.

The land was sparsely settled, the farms huge. The nearest farmhouses to ours were three, four, five miles away. It was virgin bush: a few trees had been cut for mine furnaces. Every kind of animal lived there: sable, eland, kudu, bushbuck, duiker, anteaters, wild cats, wild pigs, snakes. There were flocks of guinea fowl, partridges, hawks, eagles, pigeons, doves – birds, birds, birds. Dawns were explosions of song; the nights noisy with owls and nightjars and birds whose names we never knew; all day birds shrilled and cooed and hammered and chattered. But paradise had already been given notice to quit. The leopards and baboons had gone to the hills, the lions had wandered off, the elephants had retreated to the Zambesi Valley, the land was emptying.

But it was still a wilderness that my parents were taking on. The farm itself was approached by a disused mine track, a dirt road. The railway was seven miles away. Not one acre had been cleared for planting. The labourers were people who had been savagely defeated in a war thirty-five years before, and who left their villages and came out to work only because they had to pay the Poll Tax imposed on them precisely to make them work.

Having found their farm, my parents came back to collect

the children. Their daughter as usual had been very naughty indeed, much worse than ever before: she had lied, stolen, run away, sulked, and screamed. My mother knew it was all the fault of this travelling about: children need an ordered existence. She got us into a covered wagon drawn by twenty or so oxen, while her husband rode alongside it on his horse. The journey took five days. Inside the wagon was everything they possessed.

While the trees were being cleared off the hill where the house was to be built, we lodged at the gold mine just over the ridge.

Settlers always built themselves mud-and-thatch huts, joined by verandahs, which were expected to last only a year or so, to be replaced after the first good season by brick and tin. Our house was a single elongated hut, divided into four rooms. Its walls were of mud smeared over poles and whitewashed, the roof thatch cut from the grass in the *vleis*, the floor of stamped mud and dung.

All the floors were covered with black linoleum, and furniture was made from petrol and paraffin boxes stained black and curtained with flour sacks that were dyed and embroidered by my mother. In the front room, which had windows all around it, 'like the prow of a ship' as my mother insisted, were Persian rugs, Liberty curtains, a piano, and the heavy display silver of the period.

While my mother supervised the gang of black men building the house, my father watched the teams who cleared the bush for planting.

Then there was the business of Biddy O'Halloran, who turned out so badly. She had definitely expected something like Nairobi, and found herself stuck in this lonely and savage place with suitors of the wrong class. Every unattached male for fifty miles came visiting to propose to her, and she did not have as much time for the children as my mother thought was due. There were quarrels, and she departed back home. Then, about a year after the arrival in Africa, my mother became ill and took to her bed and stayed there. It was her heart. It is clear now that she was in an acute anxiety state, was having a breakdown. Neither her doctor in Salisbury, nor she (a nurse) could see it. The worst for her, of course, was the isolation. What my father revelled in – for he had at last found the life that suited him – was destroying her. Having always been surrounded by people, she now had only the blacks, towards whom she had had from the start all the attitudes typical of the settler: they were primitive, dirty, stupid. She was never able to see that there was anything interesting in them. Her neighbours were lower-middle class and working class, mostly Scottish, who had come out before the War and had got rich on maize. She did not want to seem snobbish, but what did she have in common with them? She had no intention of spending her life talking about gardening and recipes and dress patterns. But that was what her life now was, just like theirs.

She got out of bed, complained of a thousand aches and pains, went back again. She complained continually, and it was unlike her, for it simply wasn't done to make a fuss! She lay in a bed specially made by a neighbour who ran a timber mill, with attachments for books and magazines, and summoned her children to her throughout the day, to comfort her. 'Poor sick mummy,' she insisted, and we responded with fervent but (in my case at least) increasingly resentful embraces.

But this was certainly not all that went on at her bedside. Early childhood is when children learn best, and nothing was going to get in the way of our instruction, according to Montessori. In and out of bed, she read to us, told us stories; she was a marvellous teacher of small children. We were taught geography by means of piles of mud and sand left

120

over from the house building – making continents and countries and mountains that hardened in the sun and that, for oceans and rivers, could be filled with water. She taught us arithmetic with seeds and hens' eggs and baby chicks. She made us understand the solar system through games in which we were planets, the moon, the sun. We were made to notice stars, birds, animals. For a while we were taught by a correspondence course, but its lessons were not nearly as good as hers, and she ordered us books from England, and two periodicals whose impossibly high standards of writing would find no equal today. The *Children's Newspaper* offered news about discoveries, inventions, archaeological finds, beasts and birds, and the *Merry-Go-Round* printed stories and poems by writers like Walter de la Mare and Eleanor Farjeon. It was my mother who introduced me to the world of literature, into which I was about to escape from her.

And then my mother got herself out of bed, and went on living. She had been ill for a year. I wonder if she ever understood that her illness had been a way of denying what she knew she had to face. What courage that must have taken! I know it and I admire it, but I can't put myself in her place. It was the farm, the veld, that she hated, that trapped her. She was planning, scheming, dreaming of escaping from it, from the moment she arrived. But the farm, the veld, Africa is to me, quite simply, the luckiest thing that ever happened.

Writing about my mother is difficult. I keep coming up against barriers, and they are not much different now from what they were then. She paralysed me as a child by the anger and pity I felt. Now only pity is left, but it still makes it hard to write about her. What an awful life she had, my poor mother. But it was certainly no worse than my father's, and that is the point: he was equipped by nature for hard

121

times, and she was not. He may have been a damaged, an increasingly sick man; she was strong and full of vitality. But I am not as sorry for him as I am for her. She never understood what was happening to her.

II

In the Twenties, and even more in the Thirties, young middle-class people fled from hard times in Britain where they could not get work, to make a life in the Colonies. Often they had no money, but knew they would be given land and loans. They struggled, and very often failed. If their families at Home sent them their return fares, they went back to what they had left, degrees of genteel poverty, to be rescued, presumably, by World War II. How many of them were there? A great many, I think, for the turnover of white people, certainly in Southern Rhodesia, was always large. There is no way now of finding out about them. What a story! What stories! – and recently I read two of them, for I was sent a couple of manuscripts, memoirs by white women of their lives as white settlers, one in Kenya, one in Southern Rhodesia. These people, without any kind of training, either psychological or practical, found themselves in the bush, usually with not even an acre cleared for planting, in some kind of shack, coping with floods, droughts, fires, wild animals, and black labourers who, having been forced out to work by the Poll Tax, were sullen, angry, inefficient. Not the least of the ironies was that the whites saw themselves as pitifully poor, and the blacks saw them as unreachably rich. Both were right. Now what comes through most strongly in these accounts is that it seems, once these unsatisfactory members of the family had left Britain, it was out of sight, out of mind. The strongest and most frequent note struck is how small sums of money – £50, £25, would often have saved a situation, but money was never forthcoming. That the middle classes tend to be mean to their own is well-known, but never have I seen it so painfully shown as here. Perhaps their families did not have any money to help out with? There was no money to help my parents; all our relatives were just surviving.

These memoirs made me think about the differences between my parents and these settlers who would never have left Home if they could only have found what my father loathed so bitterly and left: a good, safe, respectable job. There were basically two kinds of immigrants: those who could not make it in Britain, and those who could, but who would not conform to British respectability. My father was one of the misfits who provided the landscape of my growing up with colourful characters whose eccentricities, suppressed in Britain, were given plenty of room to expand.

Above all, it was my mother who was defined by these women's reminiscences, all of failure, incapacity, incompetence, muddle. They could not cope with floods and fires and snakes, or having to cook bread in antheaps when the kitchen burned down, or making furniture from paraffin boxes and curtains, and dresses from flour sacks. They could not do more than just suffer what was happening to them, and of course they despised and feared the blacks. With what wails of self-pity and misery did they struggle to impose respectability on the veld, their main drive being to remain what they were – middle class; their fear being that they could become poor whites, and on the level of the blacks, just as at Home their nightmare was that they might be forced into the working class. As Denys Finch-Hatton said, as he watched the little villas of suburbia marching across the magnificent wildness of the Ngong Hills towards

Nairobi, 'This continent of Africa has a very fine sense of sarcasm.' (*Out of Africa* by Karen Blixen.)

But the fear was real enough. Very often I heard my parents say, in the troubled, grieved voice we use for those whose fate may easily be ours, 'So and so's gone bust, he's got a job as storekeeper at the mine, she's going to be a matron – ' (or governess or housekeeper) 'and God help those kids.'

Far from wailing and wincing, my mother enjoyed all the contriving and making do. They complained, 'No decent fruit here, no vegetables, our chickens die . . .' Her vegetable garden could have fed a village, and she had fruit trees, chickens, rabbits. She made cheese and the store hut was always full of preserves. She was endlessly adaptable and inventive. She had too much energy, capacity, for her situation. Her fate should have been to run a large organization, a hospital, or even an industry. On the farm she burned herself out.

Five years after we arrived on the farm, this was the situation . . . land had been cleared, and more and different crops were being grown, but we were just as much in debt to the Land Bank. The house, built to last two years, was going to have to stand much longer. Verandahs and additions of all kinds had been made. Her son, aged eight, was still being taught at home; but like all the boys of the district he spent most of his time in the bush. Her daughter, after a couple of bad choices in the way of schools, interminable and unforgettable to the child, but lasting only a few weeks and therefore unimportant to the adult, was in a convent in Salisbury. Convents are more ladylike than other schools. If my mother had known what went on, she would have removed me at once, but there is a convention that children do not tell parents about school. All she knew was that I was very homesick. These days this would be seen as a symptom of something very wrong at home; but in those unsophisticated times she was able to see it as proper and gratifying affection. She did not feel it as shocking, to send a child of seven to boarding school. At that age, children were sent Home from India to board; in England boys were sent at seven to boarding school. And what else could she have done? All the farmers' children went to school in the towns.

Her husband, not her children, was then her main worry. It is hard for the competent – and for those who have all their will behind what they do – to understand those who simply cannot make things work. My father's dreams of getting rich in five years had become a brave family joke. Besides, the Slump had begun. Long past were the days when farmers made sudden fortunes out of maize; still in the future were the fortunes made out of tobacco. Everywhere, farmers were just holding on, nursing their debts to the Government, running up bills at the grocer and the butcher, taking small risks on mixed crops, like sunflower, cotton, peanuts, sun hemp. So in any case things were against my father, but his own nature was worse. He did not really care, and I think she never understood that. War had only intensified what he was, and – from her point of view – that was bad enough. Recently a cousin sent me material about a second cousin of my father, a Victorian who was a melancholy gentleman farmer in Suffolk, writing mellow verses in the Wordsworthian manner about Death, Fate, Life and Nature. A copy is in the British Museum. He and my father even looked alike. So my mother was up against much worse than she had foreseen, though she might have remembered that his father, married to an ambitious, forceful woman, was happy as a bank clerk, spending every free moment playing the organ in the village church. Left to himself, her husband would dream his life away, content, contemplating the African night sky, sunsets, ants at work in a log, veld fires burning their slow way across the mountains in the dry season, the changing colours of the veld and, but a good way behind Nature, the fascinating improbabilities of human behaviour, white and black.

She pushed and she nagged and she made plans. Her aims were simple. Enough money must be made to pay off the debts, and then we must sell the farm and return to England where real life was waiting for her. Talk about what life would be like in England (London, of course) went on all my childhood and was referred to by my brother and myself as 'getting-off-the-farm.' Not with derision; nor did we ever sit down and analyse the nonsense of it all. It was simply too remote, this talk of good schools and nice houses, of housemaids and buses, theatres and parks.

But my father didn't want to get off the farm. Having reached England, what then? He loathed the Bank, where in any case he might not now get a job. And she could not return easily to nursing, with two children. How would they live? Never mind! All that would sort itself out, once they had got off the farm.

The pressures from my mother to do better caused my father, not to become a successful farmer, but to take a step sideways off this course, into the old dream of finding gold.

It sounds absurd, but it wasn't. The district is called Banket, after a certain type of gold-bearing reef on the Rand, identified by some early prospector. All that country is full of gold-bearing reefs, and outcrops had been prospected everywhere. My brother and I continually came on old trenches dug by some gold-seeker, or rocks where you could see how the prospector had chipped off a sample to pan. There were two gold mines not far from the farm. We could hear the mine-stamps going, day and night, from the mine just over the ridge. Prospectors came through all the time with a gun, a prospecting pan, a hammer, a corner of a sack of maizemeal, and a blanket. They came more often as the Slump deepened and they could not find work. There were many men in those days roaming the bush, self-sufficient and costing nothing, while their wives rode out the bad time as housekeeper somewhere they could have the children in the holidays. Gold was all about us, in the earth, in people's talk, in the history of this area, which was full of old diggings from when the first explorers and missionaries came in. We said they were made by the Arabs. When my father took a hammer with him on his visits around the farm, and brought back samples of rock, then crushed them in the mortar and panned them, he did no more than most farmers when they came on a likely outcrop or bit of reef. But very soon it became an obsession. Supervising the farm work took second place to gold-seeking. He was spending hours of every day stomping over the veld on his wooden leg with the hammer, and the car always came back loaded with rocks. A man was taken off farm work to pound the samples, to dig little trenches after a likely reef, to take a sample into the station to catch a train into Salisbury and the Assay Office. On mail days, when we waited for the results to come back, the tension was painful. Soon it was not trenches, but shafts that were being dug, and not one labourer but two or three were permanently on this work. My mother of course protested that if the same effort were to be put into the farm work, then . . . But nothing like this effort would have been enough to change anything in Slump time. Farmers were going bankrupt, and their land was being bought by more successful farmers, or by combines. This was the beginning of the process that created enormous units of land, hundreds of thousands of acres large, that would shortly be growing not food, but tobacco, making tobacco fortunes, the 'tobacco barons.'

And then, it was not just prospecting, but divining. My

father had discovered he could divine for water. If water, why not gold? If gold, it would not just be a question of finding a gold mine here, on this farm (and that was only a matter of time) but becoming someone to whom the big mining companies from all over the world would come rushing, demanding his services. And then he could train other people to do it, and he could start a school of divining . . .

While all this went on, my mother was trying to maintain what to her was normality. I am sure it had never occurred to her that a lively social life was something one could do without. All her best memories of girlhood, and of her years as a nurse, and then her early marriage in Persia, were of visits and parties and musical evenings and jolly times. Among – this went without saying – *nice people*. The people who farmed around us were not of our class, they had all been working-class or lower-middle-class people, most of them Scotch. While we visited them, and they us, while she performed all the functions of a neighbour, from exchanges of farm produce to helping during times of crisis, they were not what she had in mind. My brother and I did not understand what she was on about; and our father was not interested enough to enlighten us as to why so much effort had to go into keeping up friendships with people who might be living many miles away, why this was so important to her. What one did was to 'spend the day' with whatever family it was, on their farm; or they came to us; but all this was within the limits set by farmwork and the seasons and the school holidays. Some lived beyond one or two rivers which might be impassable when the rains were heavy. We started off early, so as to arrive for morning tea. The men of course talked farming, and the women hungrily talked – and talked – and talked. All the men of the district were guilty when they remembered how their wives starved for the companionship of women. There was lunch. Then tea. All the people in the district kept up the five-meals-a-day pattern of eating, which they had brought from Home. (The Africans called the whites The People Who Never Stop Eating.) In between these meals, we children went climbing *kopjes* or exploring the bush, looking for baboon troops or wild pig. After supper we drove home through the bush where all kinds of animals appeared in the headlights: the different kinds of buck, from little duiker to the big eland and kudu, wild cats, porcupines, monkeys. My brother and I fought to stay awake.

There was one thing these nice people had in common that I didn't see then. They were survivors of World War I. The men had artificial arms or legs or an eye-patch where an eye had gone. They would discuss the whereabouts of various bits of shrapnel forever travelling about their bodies out of sight, but sometimes appearing from healthy tissue to tinkle into a shaving mug or onto a plate. One woman had had four sons and a husband killed in the Trenches, and was farming with the remaining son. She was dignified, stoical, and the house was full of photographs of dead men in uniform. Another family had two boys whom we played with, but photographs of a third dominated the house and the talk of the parents: he had been drowned in a torpedoed ship. There was a man with a steel plate keeping his brains in, and another who was rumoured to have a steel plate holding in his bowels. They talked about the war, both men and women – the war, the war, the war; and we children escaped into the bush away from it, just as, at home, my brother and I tried to shut our ears against what my father came to call, sarcastically, the Great Unmentionable: 'I don't want to bore you with the Great Unmentionable, God forbid that you should waste your time on anything so unimportant.' Talk of the war was like this business of *nice people*, with which our mother continually persecuted us. The poor woman was behaving normally for her class and her time, only doing her duty as she saw it by her offspring. There we might be, at the breakfast table, the four of us. My father of course was thousands of miles away, probably in the Trenches, or in some conference of scientists, all of whom hung on his every syllable. We, the children, sitting on either side of the table, would be regarding her with expressions of embarrassed impatience, while we fidgeted to be off into the bush. 'Do listen,' she would say, 'no, just this once, *listen*. One of these days, when we get off the farm, you'll have to live with nice people, just like everybody else; you won't be racketing around with every kind of person as you do here. Michael – you talk to them! Tell them to listen to me, just this once – *Michael*!'

'What is it?' he would say. 'Oh yes, now then you kids, listen to your mother.' But he would already be up and reaching for his divining rod, and we went as fast as we could after him, trying not to see the hurt, wistful look on her face.

This business of gold, of divining, meant that the structure of visiting and being visited was always threatened. He would grumble for days at the prospect of having to go off for the day to this or that family: 'Oh *Lord*, do I have to? Oh very well, but it'll have to be Sunday, when the boys are off.' Or: 'Sorry, impossible, we'll be starting the planting, now the rains have begun.' But he thought nothing of driving thirty miles on a workday to visit some little mine so as to test out a theory on a reef. It was known exactly how the reef ran underground, where it petered out, what minerals and rock composed it, how much gold it carried. And there my father was, all day in the punishing sun, a shabby but urgent figure walking back and forth over the reef, sometimes for hours, while my mother sat politely talking with a woman she was sure she had nothing in common with, and while we kids hung about the mine which was alien to us, being farming children.

And then we drove back through the starlight, the night air coming in scented from the grasses, but chilled, so that we had to wrap up well after the long hot day. My mother, sitting there in her smart hat, with her gloves and her bag on her lap, would say: 'Well, Michael, was it worth it?'

'What, old girl? Yes, I think so.'

'We've been there all day,' she would persist, in the small unhappy voice she used when she felt that it was her duty to be stubborn, 'and there was no one keeping an eye on the farm . . .'

'But it is all information, isn't it? If that reef is going two ounces to the ton, and I was getting that degree of response, then I'll know how to measure what there is when I strike gold at our place, won't I?'

It was not their style to quarrel, shout, raise their voices, accuse or sulk. I cannot remember this ever happening. But I lay awake at night to listen to them arguing. Their voices came easily through the now cracking and loosening mud walls. My mother's voice was patient, persistent – the voice of reason. He stood his ground, but it was a very different one from hers. Her facts and figures were all small sober possibilities with the vagaries of the seasons allowed for. His talk was of great sums of money and gold-bearing reefs like glittering rivers.

In 1935, ten years after my parents arrived in the Colony, this was the situation . . . the house was still upright, a shambling old wreck, its thatch continually being repaired, the mud walls lumpy and patched. In the rainy season the roof leaked, and a bad storm sent water down in a dozen places into pails, buckets, basins. I will remember for ever a certain exquisite hammered copper basin from Persia

131

standing in the middle of the floor on a shabby but glowing Persian rug, like a picture from a fairy tale. Water dropped into it from the thatch, bringing down straws, beetles, and ants that clung to the straws, and laboured their way up them over the edges of the basin, down onto the rug, back across the floor to the walls, and so to the roof.

At the windows the Liberty curtains still hung, pretty but threadbare. In the trunk behind the curtain a dozen evening dresses bought for the fascinating social life my mother had expected to find here lay in their folds of tissue paper with mothballs, when they were not being used for 'dressing up.' My father's dress clothes lay there too, unregretted. 'Good God!' he would say, 'just imagine that people are actually prepared to climb into all those stiff collars and suits and go off to spend an evening talking rubbish to strangers they don't care tuppence about. It is hard to believe it all still goes on.' The farm was exactly as before, neither successful nor bankrupt. Every year the loan with the Land Bank was re-negotiated. When the money came in at the season's end for the crops, some of the grocer's account was paid off. If the Slump was lifting elsewhere, this did not seem to be happening here, in this district, though a couple of farmers whose fortunes had been solidly based on the maize grown for World War I were doing well. Now, in Zimbabwe, the sons of these farmers are some of the richest in the country.

My father had been talked into doing a couple of seasons of tobacco, and there were two tobacco barns to prove it. To build barns was expensive, but they were standing empty. Getting up at night at all hours to check temperatures, and the steamy air of the curing process (Virginia, not Turkish) had been too much for my father. Now he had sugar diabetes as well. If he had got this disease even a year before he did, he must have died, for insulin had only just been discovered. He had it very badly. He was supposed to eat only lean meat and lettuce and dry biscuits, for this was the diet in those early days before the doctors learned better. But my mother rebelled and said he would die of starvation before he did of diabetes. She took command and worked out with him how to adjust a variety of foods to the intake of insulin. She was, with every day, more of a nurse again. My father, like many diabetics, had become a hypochondriac. The man who had disdained to make allowances for his wooden leg, climbing trees, riding horses, going down deep mine-shafts in dangerous buckets, now talked of his symptoms with all the intensity he still put into gold and divining. From suffering and resenting the gold-fever, now my mother had become grateful that the passion existed, for it kept my father out every day at his work of divining for gold, and then he wasn't thinking about his rapidly worsening health.

By now he saw the divining as a new science, which he was founding. He used iron rods and steel rods and twigs of various woods from the bush. He 'neutralized' the gold in the reefs far under his feet with gold rings held in his hands with the ends of the rods. He tried out silver rings, nuts and bolts from the plough, brass curtain rings, or dipped the rods in water, or in solutions of various chemicals and minerals. He worked at it most of the day, and dreamed of it at night, waking my mother to say, 'Listen, old girl, if water neutralizes water, and gold, gold, then when the rod pulls down at the end of that trench there, it can't be gold or water, there's something else down there. I wonder what it can be? Chrome? Asbestos? What do you think?' Chrome and asbestos mines were not far off, and lumps of chrome and raw asbestos were part of his equipment. We loved to play with asbestos, alluring stuff, looking like those sweets called satin cushions, or like mermaid's hair, green and glittering.

I wrote about my father, disguised, in a tale called

133

Eldorado where the painful passion for gold is described. But by now gold, the lust and the itch for it, had long since become secondary. He was lost in this science of his. He believed he was creating a new method for finding any mineral, gold only one of them. He was alone in the world, so he saw it, with no one sympathetic to talk to, though the children did listen, did try out the rods, and walk with him along the trenches tracking elusive reefs when they were not at school. Only the occasional water diviner who came wandering through the farms, hoping to pick up a five pound note for finding a well, listened to him with understanding – and they started to look polite when he began talking about gold and minerals. He wondered who else, and where, in what continent and country were other people who must be pursuing this line of thought? Perhaps he could advertise in the main newspapers of the world, and make contact with them?

'No, you can *not*,' said my mother, 'we can't afford it.' Why was everyone so small-minded? One day his family would take him seriously: but then prophets are never appreciated by their nearest and dearest.

He sent for books and magazines on metals and mining, ranging from the scientific to the mystical, while my mother protested she needed the money to clothe her children. He regretted he hadn't had the foresight to study metallurgy and chemistry at school: was it too late to study by correspondence course? He brooded about the influence of the moon on metals in the earth, and the influence of metals in the earth on the moon, and on humans and animals.

Whereas once he had refused to have the scotchcart (two barrels on a frame, drawn by two oxen) bring water up the hill to the house more than twice a week, so that baths had to be rationed, now the cart made the journey every day, because so much water was needed for panning the samples.

Precious water ran away down the stony hill and made lush plantations of bright green weed among the silvery-gold grasses of the dry season. Now, not one or two samples were sent into Salisbury to be assayed, but sometimes dozens. It was all costing a fortune.

But what could my mother do? Her common sense continually outraged, she suffered and rebelled, but mostly in silence, for she, too, was alone, with no one to listen to her. She had all kinds of symptoms herself, particularly bad headaches. She knew that her heart was weak, but no one took this seriously, not even the doctors. She could sleep only when full of sedatives.

And yet . . . gold might be found, even now? Gold had been found, not three miles away, and she had gone with her Michael (for she always supported him, no matter how wrong she thought him) to test out a new theory. The miner was a middle-aged Scotchman who had already gone bankrupt several times on farms and on mines, in the way of these days. This was a last gamble, a mere single shaft in the ground, with old and rickety mine machinery. He lived on game shot in the bush, and maize porridge (just like a Kaffir!) and he had the red-eyed sullen look of the compulsive drinker. She knew herself to be lucky, compared with such as he. One day, Michael's ridiculous theories might turn out to have something in them, and then she could get off the farm . . . But what, then, would she do with such a sick husband? She had accepted that he would never be well, must get worse; and now it was her children who worried her most.

Her son she had got into the only private school in the country that could be compared with real schools in England, a prep school run along English lines. It was expensive, and of course we could not afford it. She had used all her organizing abilities to pull strings and get grants.

But what would happen to him afterwards? Nothing like an English public school was available, then there would be the question of his career. No money to set him up, no future! She wanted him to go into the Navy, and spend his life with nice people, but when she talked about it, he looked vague and off he went into the bush with his rifle, alone, or with a black boy for company.

Recently my brother came from Africa to visit, and we talked about that childhood of ours, in the old thatched mud house in the bush. A miracle of good luck! We were on land never before farmed, the bush still unspoiled by white and black idiots, surrounded by every kind of wild animal and bird, free to wander as we wanted over thousands of acres, solitude the most precious of our gifts . . . but our mother lay awake at night, ill with grief because her children were deprived, were not good middle-class children in some suburb in London.

If her son's future was an anxiety, then what could she say about her daughter!

I was always ill at school. Now I know I was ill with homesickness. I did have a couple of real illnesses, malaria and dysentery, but I acquired with my mother's connivance vague ailments that were always taking me into the convent sickroom with the need to be cosseted. My mother would make her reluctant husband rush her the seventy miles into town – the word 'rush' here is relative: in our ancient Overland the trip took hours. There she informed the nuns and the doctor that I must have this or that kind of treatment: she knew best, she had been trained at the Royal Free, in London. When I was actually in the classroom, I did well enough, but the pressure of my mother's need that I should be cleverer than anyone else was intense, and I was trying to escape from it. Her schemes for my future had the illusory poisoned glow of the gold-mining talk which by then

I refused to listen to. The music lessons I took must end on concert platforms, because she could have been a concert pianist. If I hummed a tune, grand opera was waiting for me. Talk of great painters accompanied my attempts at drawing. All this was in English terms. It was inconceivable that I, or any other white child, should learn Shona, or try to understand the lives of Africans. It is impossible to believe now, but a man who travelled around making recordings of African music was considered a Kaffir-lover and a traitor to the whites. A poet who lived in the bush, befriending Africans and liked by them, was hated by the whites, who responded to any mention of him with that loud, uneasy, derisive laughter that means people are feeling threatened. What is the use of exclaiming: 'But that's insane!' It was how things were.

I did also write little pieces. But I hid these attempts from her, because I felt that they weren't mine, but hers; for she took possession of them, talking about them to everyone.

When I was fourteen I finally slid out of school on a pretext and stayed on the farm, where I lay on my bed reading, or went about the bush with my rifle. I was supposedly ill with 'low fever.' Perhaps I did have it. I certainly had a permanent low temperature, lacked energy, and was dosed with quantities of quinine that I am amazed didn't kill me. But there came a rescue. I was sent on a two months' holiday by a charitable organization to another part of the country, right away from home. There I saw certain things very clearly. One was that there was nothing wrong with me. I knew I had to escape from that house where both parents were ill, obsessed with illness. When I went home I told my mother that I was very well, and said, 'It's no good trying to make me ill, ever again.' Of course she did not know what I meant, believed that I was, as always, cruel and unfair.

I think now that she was a bit crazy with the menopause. These days she would be given a few pills and remain her normal, humorous, moderate self. She was obsessed. With the deficiencies of her black servants, for one thing. Like nearly all the white housewives then (and now, it goes on still, in South Africa) she spoke to them in a nagging voice full of dislike, much to the distress of my father. 'What's the point of making people just out of their villages fuss about teaspoons and cups and saucers that match?' Most of the time she listened, but now she cried: 'I suppose you want me to lower my standards!' And she was obsessed with me: my brother was at school and safely out of the way. Everything I was, and did, shocked her. She wanted me to remain a little girl, in a country where girls grew up early. Because she insisted that I wear childish clothes, I earned the money to buy material by shooting guinea fowl and doves for the local butcher and I made my own clothes. They were grown-up clothes and she hated them. I was reading books that I found for myself, no longer the classics and the 'good' children's books she ordered for me. I was critical about what I saw around me, the poverty of the blacks, the attitudes of the whites, but in a confused, uninstructed way, and this left me vulnerable to her. But what was really making her ill with frustration was that she needed to project all her energies and talents into her daughter, who would live, for her, the life she had been prevented from living. But the girl had become a sullen, angry wall of rejection, usually silent, and then cracking into rudeness and derision.

'Why do you hate me so much?' she would cry; while I complained to my father, 'Why does she hate me? She has always hated me.'

Now I understand her state of mind very well. She was afflicted by that common disease of middle life, feeling that everything was slipping through her fingers; she could not grasp hold of or retain anything. Or as if she were juggling far too many balls in the air, and knew that if she dropped one they would all come clattering down.

I put an end to the awfulness of being at home with her by going off to Salisbury and becoming what is now known as an au pair. (This used to mean rich families in different countries exchanging daughters so that they could learn the language and the customs.) I did this in two different families for eighteen months. It was boring, not too bad; the people were pleasant, everyone got on. But it was a waste of time, and my mother was desperate because her daughter was a nursemaid. This rage and misery of hers reached me wherever I was in very long letters full of improbable threats, such as that I was bound to end up in the brothels of Beira. I had no defence against a mother I could not recognize, except to become cold and indifferent. I went back home to the farm to write a novel. I was the apotheosis of a difficult adolescent. Now I am appalled at how I treated them both – though I could not have done differently. For them it must have been intolerable. For me it was intolerable. I finished and tore up two bad novels and went into Salisbury, and got a job in the Central Telephone Exchange. My mother experienced this as a final defeat: her daughter was a common telephone operator. The life she was leading (not that she told her parents anything, it was necessary to go into Salisbury and make enquiries) was 'fast,' cheap, and nasty.

III

What I was doing was working all day, dancing or going to the pictures at night, and reading every minute I could. Together with all the other young people of the town (white, of course), I was in a state of accelerating excitement and elation because of the now rapidly approaching war. I see now that we were all rather mad.

When I did go home I found my mother nursing a very sick man. His divining rods hung on the walls, unused. Gold had been found on the farm, but not by him. Nothing very remarkable: a prospector was trying to make pay a reef that ran a few pennyweights to the ton, but it was galling someone else had found it. Galling to my mother. It did not occur to my father to be envious, he was pleased. But he was abstracted and vague and needed more and more to be tactfully brought back from the horrific landscapes of World War I – when he would almost certainly begin talking about the imminent World War II. He and my mother had known it was coming for years. I often wonder what combination of circumstances made them so certain, and on the whole so right, about the politics of Britain. Years before most people, for instance, they knew that Churchill was the only possible saviour for Britain. But while they talked so much sense about home politics, the international scene was a different thing. My father had become a British Israelite. He believed a large number of frightening and contradictory things. Of course my mother did not go along with this talk of Russia and Germany being anti-Christ and destined to ally themselves against Britain, which was scheduled by God to save the world. She did not like Gog and Magog and the Lost Tribe and the seven million dead around Jerusalem. She treated it as a symptom of his illnesses, and put her energies into trying to find ways to save her daughter, a flibbertigibbet who thought of nothing but men, and to get her son into the British Navy.

Very soon, the impossible girl who had said she would not marry for years, talking of a hundred (all unsuitable) careers, came home with a man she said she was going to marry at

140

once. She was nineteen, far too young, he was ten years older than she – and therefore ought to have more sense, said Michael. But this son-in-law – so enquiries elicited – was not too bad, once granted it was possible to marry a Colonial instead of a nice doctor or solicitor in England. It seemed that he had a future in the Civil Service. (In fact he ended up as Master of the High Court, with various other high official posts.) But what was intolerable to my mother was that I never mentioned any of the facts in his favour, and seemed to be quite surprised to hear them. As if these things were unimportant, irrelevant!

My mother's sense of occasion was being starved . . . again. How little would have been needed to satisfy it – as I see now. Her nature, her upbringing, demanded properly prepared for and conducted Birthdays, Anniversaries, Weddings, Jubilees. But it was her fate to have a family who temperamentally were indifferent. Her husband did not remember birthdays, and when she did, would give her that long, thoughtful, interested look which meant she was being found petty again. 'Birthdays,' he could be heard thinking, 'Why should anybody care about them? Just another silly convention!' 'Oh, our anniversary is it? Oh Lord, I'm sorry, well, if you really think we ought to . . .' And now her daughter only said, 'This is Frank Wisdom, we're getting married next month.' It never crossed her mind to get engaged, or to want an engagement ring. Almost at once there was a slapdash and graceless wedding which made my mother miserable.

Then two things happened. Germany invaded Poland, and war was declared; simultaneously the young couple announced that there was going to be a grandchild, but on no account was there to be any fuss about it. There was a war on and, in any case, he was going to be sent up North to fight.

My mother longed to fuss and knit and sew and talk about pregnancies, but when she did, she was merely tolerated. All her natural feelings were being blocked, again. This was not the only way she was being frustrated. A declaration of war is certainly an Occasion, which demands, by convention, certain responses, and she was responding accordingly. All this time on the farm, even when most beset by worry, at her poorest, she had always behaved as upbringing said she should, raising money for good causes, trying to form committees. And now, with the war starting, she rallied her neighbours into various kinds of war work. She was resented for it: Who does she think she is? – was being asked, and by no means for the first time.

But she had succeeded in getting my brother, Harry, into the Navy in England. This had not been easy, and all kinds of strings had had to be pulled: only because it was wartime was it possible at all. Once my brother was actually in Dartmouth he found it hard to keep up: he had not had it in his mind to be in the Navy in the first place, had always wanted to be a farmer. He did not have all the subjects needed for the Navy, and had to study harder than the others.

But he was there. At last something good was happening, something appropriate, linking her with her upbringing and her old hopes – and for the first time since she had come to this country. Where she still did not feel at home. But she no longer talked of going back Home. In wartime it was not possible: who could say how long the war would last? And her children would be here, for her son said he would come back the minute he could, Africa was where he belonged, and her daughter was married here. Satisfactorily married: even if *how* she did everything was wrong, and calculated only (my mother was convinced) to hurt her, what she was doing was no more than the colonial equivalent of what she herself would have liked, and should have done.

For a while it seemed as if this marriage could not really begin until after the war, but then it turned out Frank was not going up North with the others, he was medically unfit. A house was being bought. She was not consulted about the house, though she knew exactly what they needed and should have: plenty of room for children and for entertaining. And they bought such a house. It was in one of the old avenues full of trees, a bungalow in an already outmoded style with rooms spreading about and verandahs and an enclosed back verandah.

The first child was born, and of course the young couple had no idea of how to handle the baby. It was her duty to put things right . . .

My mother did not learn to drive until she left the farm. I found that strange. True that it was rarer then for older women to drive, but plenty did. It was just something she did not, would not, do. As brave as she was I did not believe she was afraid. A woman who thought nothing of holding a revolver straight to a cobra's head to blow it off? It was a mystery . . . but, not knowing how to drive meant that her husband and her children had to drive her about, and it was one way of getting help and support from them: they gave her so little.

The more she brooded about the bad state of affairs in her daughter's house in town, the more often she decided she must go in and take a look. Now that her husband was too ill to drive all that way, she had to find lifts. The day before a trip she spent roasting chickens, making cakes, jam, peanut butter, lemon curd, ginger beer. The neighbour's car would be loaded to the roof with all this stuff. She usually did not ring her daughter before coming, because she was afraid of something new in her: a cool, smiling, impervious politeness. As recently as three years ago the girl had been rude, sullen, tactless – impossible; now she was polite – and impossible. If informed that her mother would be arriving next day, she would certainly be polite, but say she was going to be away or busy or something.

My mother would arrive with food of every kind. She found the larder and refrigerator full. The house was just like every other, at that time. The cookboy was in the kitchen, peeling vegetables. The houseboy, having finished his work by ten in the morning, was probably gossiping with friends at the back in the sanitary lane. The 'piccanin' was playing with a toy in the garden or on guard over the pram with the baby in it. And where was her daughter? She might be cooking: she enjoyed that, and husbands came home for lunch. Or she might be visiting with the wives of her husband's colleagues. This seemed to my mother a suitable occupation, proof that I was growing up. At last. Ever since she had been in the Colony she had longed for visits with women – morning tea parties, afternoon tea parties, real companionship with nice women. But her daughter might easily explode with, 'If I have to sit through another bloody tea party with bloody gossiping women complaining about their servants, I'll slit my throat.' And then seem to remind herself, and pull tight the reins of politeness, putting a smile on her face and offering tea and cake.

My mother would go into the kitchen to check shelves, saucepans, and whether the tea and sugar had been stolen. She spoke sharply to the cook, who went off in a huff. She summoned the houseboy to do a room over again. She complained that it was dangerous to let the 'piccanin' touch the baby, because of the germs. She reorganized various bits of furniture to her satisfaction and then, worn out with it all, sat down, lit a cigarette, and waited for a real conversation to begin. But, as she could see, her daughter was being unreasonable again – angry, where she ought to be grateful. Not that she showed she was angry: she sat smiling, smiling

144

if it killed her, and said nothing. Once after a really good going-over of the entire house, she heard her daughter say to the cook: 'I am sorry about my mother. She is an old woman. Take no notice.' She was furious. In the first place she was not old. And she *knew* that the servants took advantage, did as they liked, and the young people had all kinds of silly ideas, paid the lazy black people far too much. She wanted to talk it all over, to have real serious discussions about it all, so that they would listen, and see how wrong they were. She had had experience of servants in England, in Persia, and now here!

She would come rushing into town planning these conversations in her mind: there were a thousand things that needed discussing, quite apart from the upbringing of the baby, and the servants. Everything about that household disturbed her, and it was her daughter's fault: and yet no one could say the girl was lazy. The pantry was full of jams and preserves made by her. There were always guests and a great deal of trouble was taken over food. She made her own clothes (including far too many dance dresses: surely there was no need for them to go out dancing quite so much?) – all her baby's clothes, and her husband's shirts and pyjamas. Why did she not ask her mother to help her? Why did she always say no – politely, of course – to any offers of help? Why did she not understand that her mother's life had always been sacrificed to her and to her brother; a mother's duty is to sacrifice herself to her children . . .

Women of that generation talked easily about sacrificing themselves, to children who were patient, ironical, or rude. A revolution had not taken place: the one that would have informed her that her daughter's terrible homesickness at school was a bad thing; that some of her own symptoms might not have physical causes; that one did not talk about 'sacrificing oneself' . . .

But it *was* her duty to sacrifice herself, no matter how much, and how unfairly, she was misunderstood; and she got lifts in from the farm quite often. But it was getting difficult because of petrol rationing. She saw it was time to move into town, particularly as there was going to be another baby, much too soon of course! But what an anticlimax, what a defeat! 'Getting off the farm' – that dream full of gold dust and magic – was it really going to become an affair of tamely selling the farm (not too badly, because of the war) and buying a house in town? A house, a mere box of a place, was bought. There wasn't enough money to buy something really nice, once the Land Bank was paid off. And the house was not in the centre, but in a suburb several years off being fashionable. My father was moved in, hating every minute. He did not want to leave the farm, the veld, the space – what he had come to Africa to find. He kept saying there was nothing left for him now, but to die. My mother protested that it was not as bad as that! – but knew it was, very bad. She felt that their lives were ending before they had really begun, for the time on the farm did not really count. She had always been waiting for life to begin when she could move off it.

My brother, Harry, was on the *Repulse* in the Pacific with the *Prince of Wales*, when both ships, supposed to be unsinkable, were sunk in minutes by Japanese bombers. My brother was not drowned, though he nearly was. He was picked up out of the water where he had been floating for some hours, and sent off to Ceylon on recuperative leave. He was soon back in the fighting, in the Mediterranean.

This was very bad for my mother, who blamed herself: why was it she was punished for everything she did? It had seemed such a triumph to get her son into the Navy.

And my father seemed unable to think about anything but the war; sometimes it sounded as if it were he on that ship in the Mediterranean. A good thing he was in town near doctors and hospitals, even though he did hate this house so much. There was nothing wrong with it, my mother bravely insisted, the rooms were quite a decent size, with high ceilings; there were verandahs, there was coolness. But it was no good, he was a bitter, angry, sorrowful, not in years an old man, for he was just into his sixties, but he looked so old, so worn out, and frail. Everything was wrong with him now, and my mother could not leave him for more than half a day.

She knew that this was how it was going to be until he died. Her new life was organized with her usual energy, and courage. Money was short, and soon she was growing vegetables again, and sold them, and had chickens and ducks and sold their eggs. In spite of her husband's illness she was much more cheerful. The long isolation of the farm, which had so starved her gregarious nature, was over. She had friends in Salisbury: she always made friends easily. And there were hundreds of thousands of men in the Air Force camps around Salisbury, and they were homesick and bored. The sons of friends in England soon became visitors, and their friends too. The house was soon full of people and she looked after them, cooked enormous meals and wrote letters to their mothers. She also took on war work.

But her main occupation was, and had to be, her husband, who soon was not getting dressed at all, but lived in his dressing gown, and then took to his bed and did not ever again leave it.

He lay in a room chosen because its windows overlooked what was to him nothing but a painful reminder of what the veld, the bush, ought to be. Town veld, he called it, with far too many people threatening the long grasses, where they made innumerable paths, and the trees, which they were always cutting down. He lay propped up, gaunt and white-faced, and cups of milk slipped through his shaking hands, and if he reached for a pill from among the batteries of bottles on the medicine table near his bed, more likely than not bottles and pills scattered everywhere. He could not be left alone at all, and my mother had to give up war work and visiting, and stay with him.

It had seemed that things could hardly be worse. Then, suddenly, her daughter announced she was going to leave her husband and children. This was of course not possible. Such things were not done. But it was happening. She did not get on with Frank, said this terrible, painful, destructive girl – yet she had shown every sign of getting on with him for four years. She could not stand the life, she said; she hated everything about it.

'What does that have to do with it?' demanded the poor woman. 'We are not put into this world to please ourselves!'

Not only was the child leaving her husband (but one really ought to stop calling her a child, at twenty-three), she was running around the town with the Communists.

My mother had not known there were any Communists here, in Africa. Unable, as usual, to find out anything from the girl herself, she went visiting all around the town to get information, and found that these Communists were all foreigners, Jews, refugees, and members of the Air Force, a lot of them lower-class people. If they were Rhodesians, they were obviously misfits. Also, there was a certain corporal who had 'stolen your daughter away from her husband. A terrible thing, the way all these marriages are breaking up, but what can you expect, with all our own men up North fighting in the desert, and all these Air Force men stationed here?'

Confronted with the corporal, the girl simply laughed and

said *of course* she was not leaving her husband for a man, but for the sake of a new society. She then proceeded to deliver what she called 'an analysis' of the situation in language that was quite incomprehensible. She had often enough attacked the white way of life angrily, rudely – and of course unfairly. But what she had said had at least been understandable. Now she had acquired a new vocabulary with her new ideas.

What was happening was appalling. The way it was happening was – again – impossible. For again no one was behaving as they should. When she went to her son-in-law to apologize for her daughter's behaviour, she discovered the couple were 'seeing each other' – whatever that could mean; and that she was 'seeing' her children. My mother understood by this that the marriage might be healed, and behaved accordingly. But when she visited her daughter, she was in a dingy bed-sitting-room, had got a job as a typist, and was earning so little she could not possibly even eat properly on it. She looked ill, and soon she was ill, in bed, reading Communist books and being visited by her new Communist friends who – astonishingly – seemed quite normal people.

Appealed to for judgement – for satisfactory arrangements of words – my father said irritably that he was not at all surprised. She had been much too young to get married in the first place.

My mother badly needed some kind of ritual throwing-out of the wicked one, condemnation, then contrite tears, then complaints of ill-treatment or of suffering. But nothing like this ever happened, and she could get no sense even out of the mistreated husband.

We talk perennially about the generation gap. But has there ever been a greater gap than between my parents' generation and mine? They believed that the British Empire was the greatest force for good in the world, and that God

149

thought so too. That white people were superior to all nonwhite races, and that British white people were superior to other white people. That the white minority in the Colonies was there with God's approval to civilize and uplift the natives. They believed in Duty. In Patriotism. In doing a job well for the sake of doing it. In staying married. In family life.

What we believed about the British Empire – or any other Empire – and about racism, sexism, inequality, and so on, has become the new orthodoxy, and there is no need to outline it. But at that particular time in the war, perhaps because of its awfulness, we believed (our particular kind of young person, and there were – briefly – a lot of us) that very soon, after the war, the whole world would voluntarily choose communism, because of its obvious and evident merits; that war would cease to exist; that the State in every country would 'wither away' of its own accord; that (probably within about ten years) there would be a worldwide Golden Age without poverty, injustice, unhappiness of any kind whatsoever.

If my parents had known what was in my head, they would have believed me mad; and I now agree with them. But in addition to the above heady set of Articles of Faith, I personally held some pretty amazing beliefs, generated in me by that long, long nightmare, watching the slow grinding down of my parents. I knew that when I stepped out of the marriage I would be breaking some dark line of Fatality, invisible but invincible, which had forced my father, once healthy, strong, handsome, to become a querulous, war-broken man waiting to die at sixty; had changed my mother from a strong, clever, competent woman into an ailing, neurotic, unhappy one. My leaving the marriage would save my children from following this road, as if I were carrying some kind of gene, not physical, but psychological; or as if I were carrier of an illness that needed decades to reveal itself.

These thoughts were shared with no one at all, though I knew when I sat by my father, holding his hand, that he would understand me at once, if I actually put into words what I felt.

Very soon the worst became worse for my mother when the delinquent married again, in the same casual, cheerful way as she did the first time, one of the refugees she was running around with. But he was a German! A German in the middle of a war against Germany! An Enemy Alien. Enquiries elicited that this new son-in-law was 'well-connected,' even if he was partly Jewish. She could have done worse, if she insisted on marrying a foreigner. When accused of deliberately trying to make them miserable by marrying an enemy, all she said was that since he was a refugee, surely it was obvious he was anti-Hitler? The man himself was dismaying, the epitome of foreignness, even Prussian, being cold, correct, and formal. It was impossible, ever, to know what he was thinking. He was like Conrad Veidt. Why, why, why, this man? You couldn't imagine a greater contrast between the two: this slow, cold, formal man, and a lively quick energetic humorous young woman – so my mother had heard her daughter described, though she had certainly never experienced her like this. This unlikely couple soon announced a new pregnancy, and it was no use asking, 'What was the point of leaving Frank and the children if you were going to get pregnant again almost at once?' 'You don't understand, Mother!'

No, she did not; and her husband did not. He seemed to see this new awfulness as only another manifestation of the general destructiveness, part of the war, part of what had to be expected in wartime. And no, he would not 'talk' to the girl; when had that done any good?

The new baby was born, healthy and fine, like the others, and he at once became a favourite of his grandfather, who lay feebly in bed with the child near him, dying interminably, knowing he was, and hating it.

My poor mother yearned for support in that long dying. Her son, perhaps, would give it? He had returned from the war rather deaf from the gunfire in many sea battles. He was slow and smiling and polite and rather absentminded, and he would not talk about the fighting. In fact, he was in a state of shock, as combatants are after a war. He did help her, but not in the way she so badly needed, someone taking responsibility off her, someone understanding what she was going through. He was thinking of getting married, was not much at home.

The new son-in-law Gottfried was always ready to advise about money. He was very good at it: one of the things she had given up trying to understand was how a Communist could be so worldly-wise. But she had no daughter. Of course, this new couple, Gottfried and Doris, would at once come when asked to sit with the dying man, so that she might go off and have a bit of a rest, or go shopping. But there was never any ease in it, never anything she could take for granted . . . she did not know what she would do without them, but it was as if they were kindly neighbours, ready to do a good turn, and this terrible ordeal of a dying man who needed nursing twenty-four hours a day was her problem and not theirs too.

Again, she was up against more than she could imagine.

The group of people I spent my time with shared many assumptions that were never examined, and only some of them were political. What seems remarkable now is how much we did share, coming from so many different countries, different social classes. We all agreed about the family, not yet called 'nuclear.' To get free of our parents had been our most urgent task, and most of us had been out earning a living very early. It would have been inconceivable for any of us to live at home with parents. Parents had to be resisted in every way and at all times, not only because they were reactionary (this went without saying) but because they wanted to live our lives for us. The tyrannical father of the last century had been defeated, but had been replaced by the mothers, who were tyrants of the emotions. All the young women I was with had problems with their mothers. We had to fight them: they were leeches who sucked the life out of us. We had all cut free but one, and she was a poor victim, always ill, whose energies were spent not on her husband, but on her formidable mother who never left her alone. But we all knew – by all here I mean our men, as well as the women – what the problem was and how it should be cured. These punishing and pathetic mothers had in their time all been special in some way, had supported the Suffragettes, fought for a career. But had been defeated. Well, it was simple! 'Come the Revolution' – (a *mot* which for some reason was being used with increasing irony), there would be proper creches and nurseries and legislation, and this phenomenon of middle-aged women being left high and dry with nothing to do but live through their children would no longer exist.

Meanwhile we – the young women – were frightened. What was to stop us becoming like our mothers? Clearly, strength of will was not enough.

What bothers me now is that my thoughts are not much more evolved than they were then. On the one hand there was this poor woman who – through no fault of her own, and because of one misfortune after another, beginning with the death of her mother when she was three – deserved love, support, cherishing. But on the other hand she had to be fought every minute, otherwise she would have swallowed me up. The thoughts revolve: around and around they go.

But I do see certain ironical aspects I did not then. One is that the Africans on whose behalf we were supposedly fighting would not have understood one word of all this. Old people were respected, and families and clans helped each other; and the idea that an elderly woman with a dying husband could be accused of emotional blackmail because she demanded help would have seemed ridiculous. But that was *then*, before white civilization had done its work.

The war ended. The men who had gone up North – those who had not been killed – came home. They were in a state of shock. The hundreds of thousands of Air Force men departed to Britain. Southern Rhodesia became itself again, except that many Italian ex-prisoners of war elected to stay. Greeks arrived, escaping from the civil war in Greece. A great many Afrikaners came in to settle. Was this really still a British Colony? For people like my mother it was, of course; it had to be.

Her son married.

Her husband died. On the Death Certificate it should have said: Of the First World War.

She was a widow. Both children exhorted her to marry again. This was cruel of them and, no, she did not suppose they meant well: they were afraid of her being a burden. How could one marry again when one had been so completely married once? Whether to the man one ought to have married (who of course was the young doctor who drowned in the First World War) or to someone else – it didn't matter: she had been married for thirty or so years to the father of her children. Yes, she did remember how, earlier, on the farm, sitting outside the house of an evening looking at the sunset, or watching the stars (the time and the place for these discussions) she had said, talking of her own stepmother who was living alone in a suburb of London, but wanting (as Maude and Michael knew quite well) to come and live on the farm in Africa, 'I am not going to be a burden on my children, I hope I die before then.'

But she was in her mid-sixties, strong, full of energy.

Both children urged her to accept the invitations she had to work for organizations such as the Red Cross. Yes, she knew she was good at it, of course she was, but she didn't want to work in some impersonal thing, she wanted to be with her family: it was the duty of women to sacrifice themselves for . . .

But her daughter really did not seem to need her at all. She still spent her time in this group of people, all Communists and Kaffir-lovers, who never seemed to be out of each other's company. Any time of the day or night, anywhere they lived (for Doris and Gottfried always seemed to be moving), their place was full of people – people talking, talking; they never stopped. Gottfried worked a lot. He had two jobs, one in a lawyer's office, and one at the Tobacco Auctions. He was paid badly in both: exploited, it seemed, because he was a German and a refugee: but that was the kind of thing they *would* say. Her daughter worked part-time, and was earning quite well, and the new baby went to a creche and throve on communal living. Offers of help were seldom accepted.

Her son did not seem to need her either: the young wife was as efficient and hardworking as she was herself.

Then, she was told this second marriage was going to end in divorce. Thank God poor Michael was dead and could not have his heart broken over the new tragedy. Which, however, was not being treated as a tragedy. Not only were the divorcing pair the best of friends, but actually went on living in the same house while the divorce went through. And what could one make of a scene where, on a picnic, Frank the first husband, with the two children, and the new stepmother, and the second husband and the new baby and the girl herself all behaved as if nothing much were happening. Nothing was said, nothing explained, no one ever told her anything: or if they did, she couldn't believe her ears.

Her daughter went off to England with the baby, refusing offers of help, either in money (not that there was much) or from relatives there. Gottfried, it seemed, would soon follow.

Very well, she would go to England too. To go Home like this, as an old woman with very little money, and no place or use there, trailing after a daughter who had never been anything else but a source of pain, when for all those years on the farm she had dreamed of how she would go back and take up where she had left . . . well, life was a funny business, as Michael always used to say.

She sold up everything in Salisbury, bought herself a typewriter, and taught herself to type. She would become her daughter's secretary.

There were reasons why she would be pleased to leave. The first novel, *The Grass Is Singing*, had come out. She was embarrassed by it. Of course they would admire that kind of thing in England, but it was wrongheaded and unfair to the whites. People were being tactful, but she could imagine what was being said behind her back. Leaving Southern Rhodesia she would be leaving, too, memories of her Michael's interminable illnesses, the failure of the farm, and the never-ending unpleasantness provided by her daughter. And now there were short stories appearing, every bit as bad as the novel. Never mind, she would live with her daughter, or near her, and sacrifice her life . . .

Two years later she returned to Southern Rhodesia. She had been frozen out. By the climate; for she had forgotten how awful it could be. And by her daughter who just would not accept help, she would not – and yet she needed it, anyone could see that.

She settled near her son. Soon, she died of a heart attack. It was as so often happens when old people die: everyone knows they need not have died at all, if only there had been something real for them to do; if they had felt wanted, needed, by someone.

On Other Writers

Afterword to
The Story of an African Farm
by Olive Schreiner

A new novel, *The Story of an African Farm*, was being discussed around London in 1883. The writer, a Mr Ralph Iron, was unknown. South Africa was still a long way off, a land of native risings, Kaffir wars, wild animals. Missionaries and explorers went there, and young men looking for adventure. Africa, large parts of it still unmapped, was the setting for tales of danger – and imagination. In his preface Ralph Iron wrote: 'It has been suggested by a kind critic that he would better have liked the little book if it had been a history of wild adventure; of cattle driven into inaccessible *kranzes* by Bushmen; "of encounters with ravening lions, and hair-breadth escapes." This could not be. Such works are best written in Piccadilly or in the Strand . . .' Also, and gently enough, he asked for a broader sympathy from a habit of criticism whose weakness was – and still is – a partiality for 'the charm that hangs about the ideal representation of familiar things.' One may profitably think about the nature of the society, safe, ordered, stable or believed to be so by that part of it who so experience it; but more profitably about the writer who understood the readers, and the critics, he hoped to engage, so well that he could choose such apposite words, and who, in rejecting stronger ones, was already showing such strength and maturity.

The novel had had a hard birth, refused by one publisher after another. Not only was it about an Africa unfamiliar to

161

England, but it had an unmarried mother whom the author refused to provide with a wedding ring. Then Chapman and Hall took it on the advice of George Meredith. Cuts and changes were suggested, and some made: it is said with resentment.

Soon it leaked out that Ralph Iron was a woman, and a young one: she was not yet thirty. She had been a governess in the Cape. She was lodging in London. She was very pretty and vivacious. Attractive female authors were then a rarity. She was around and about in London society for a while. It was not only Meredith who recognized the novel. An extraordinary assortment of the remarkable people of her time praised it. It was one of the best novels in the English language. It was greater than *The Pilgrim's Progress*. It had genius. It had splendour. For the rest of her life she was the famous author of this novel that she had written in her early twenties. And, until she died, people from every part of the world would come up to her and say that it had changed their lives. Some claim that it would have made no difference if she had never written another word. This is true, from the point of view of literature; but there were other sides to her.

Now I must write personally; but I would not, if I didn't know that nothing we can say about ourselves is personal. I read the novel when I was fourteen or so; understanding very well the isolation described in it; responding to her sense of Africa the magnificent – mine, and everyone's who knows Africa; realizing that this was one of the few rare books. For it is in that small number of novels, with *Moby Dick*, *Jude the Obscure*, *Wuthering Heights*, perhaps one or two others, which is on a frontier of the human mind. Also, this was the first 'real' book I'd met with that had Africa for a setting. Here was the substance of truth, and not from England or Russia or France or America, necessitating all kinds of mental translations, switches, correspondences, but reflecting what I knew and could see. And the book became part of me, as the few rare books do. A decade or so later, meeting people who talked of books, they talked of this one, mentioning this or that character, or scene; and I discovered that while I held the strongest sense of the novel, I couldn't remember anything about it. Yet I had only to hear the title, or 'Olive Schreiner,' and my deepest self was touched.

I read it again, for the first time as an experienced reader, able to judge and compare – and criticize. The first shock was that Olive Schreiner, who had always felt so close, like a sister, could have been my grandmother. The second was that, if I used the rules that turn out a thousand good forgettable novels a year, let the book spread out from the capsuled essence of it I had held, so that it became a matter of characters and a plot, it was not a good novel. But, then, of course, neither is *Wuthering Heights*. Well, then, what are these rules? Faced with one of the rare books, one has to ask such questions, to discover, again, that there aren't any. Nor can there be; the novel being that hybrid, the mixture of journalism and the *Zeitgeist* and autobiography that comes out of a part of the human consciousness which is always trying to understand itself, to come into the light. Not on the level where poetry works, or music, or mathematics, the high arts; no, but on the rawest and most workaday level, like earthworms making new soil where things can grow. True lovers of the novel must love it as the wise man in the fable did the crippled beauty whose complaint against fate was that she was beautiful – for what use was her beauty? She was always trying for humanity and failing. And he replied that it was because of the trying that he loved her.

The true novel wrestles on the edge of understanding, lying about on all sides desperately, for every sort of experience, pressing into use every flash of intuition or correspondence, trying to fuse together the crudest of materials, the humblest, which the higher arts can't include. But it is precisely here, where the writer fights with the raw, the intractable, that poetry is born. Poetry, that is, of the novel: appropriate to it. *The Story of an African Farm* is a poetic novel; and when one has done with the 'plot' and the characters, that is what remains: an endeavour, a kind of hunger, that passionate desire for growth and understanding, which is the deepest pulse of human beings.

There was nothing unconscious about Olive Schreiner's method, as this letter to Havelock Ellis shows. The book she discusses is her *From Man to Man*.

One thing I am glad of is that it becomes less and less what you call 'art' as it goes along. My first crude conceptions are always what you call 'art.' As they become more and more *living* and real, they become what I call higher art, but what you call no 'art' at all. I quite understand what you meant, but I cannot think that your use of the word in that sense is right, i.e., not misleading, and therefore *untrue*. If I understand what you mean, *Wilhelm Meister* is not art, one of Balzac's novels is. *Wilhelm Meister* is one of the most immortal deathless productions of the greatest of the world's artists, the result of twenty years labour, worth any six of Balzac's novels, great and glorious as Balzac is. Yet if you were writing of it, you would, ridiculous as it would seem, be *obliged* to call it 'not art.' You seem to say 'I will call "art" only that artistic creation in which I can clearly *see* the artist manufacturing the parts and piecing them together; when I cannot see that, though the thing be organic, true, inevitable, like a work of God's, I will not call it art; I must see the will shaping it (of course

164

there always has been a will shaping it, whether it is visible or not) or I will not call it art.' This of course is not in justification of my method but touches what seems to me a weakness and shallowness in your mode of criticism. It *is* very valuable that the two kinds of art should be distinguished, but not that the one should be called art and the other not art. It would be better to call the one artificial and the other real art. But that wouldn't be just. I should rather call the one organic, and the other inorganic.

And in reply to his answer: 'No, I deny that you can see how *Wilhelm Meister* was made; you can see how it *grew*, not how it was made. . . It came like that, like a tree, not like a Greek temple. You never know where you are going to turn next in *Wilhelm Meister*. No more did Goethe – yet all was of necessity, nothing of chance.'

The 'plot.' On a Karroo farm in the second part of last century, lived a widowed Dutchwoman, Tant' Sannie. There is a daughter, Em, who will inherit the farm, and a niece, Lyndall. Em is sweet, gentle, humble, 'womanly.' Lyndall is all beauty, fire, and intelligence. She is an orphan. Lyndall dreams of an education: knowledge frees. She will make the Dutchwoman send her to school. The saintly German overseer has a son, Waldo. He and Lyndall love each other as prisoners may do. To the farm comes a mountebank, Bonaparte Blenkins, who tricks the rich Dutchwoman into wanting to marry him. While under his spell she treats Waldo and his father abominably: he wants to get rid of them. Also, he enjoys cruelty. He is afraid of Lyndall, who sees through him. Discovered by Tant' Sannie making love to her much richer niece, he leaves in disgrace. Time passes. The girls are grown to marriageable age: Em is a 'yellow-haired little woman of sixteen.' A new arrival, Gregory Rose, who has hired part of the farm, is in love with her. But Em tells him that when Lyndall arrives back from her boarding school he will see a really beautiful woman, a princess, and change his mind. This happens. Lyndall despises the womanish Gregory, and spends her time with the 'low, coarse' fellow Waldo. He listens, she talks, mostly about the humiliating position of woman in her time. 'A little bitterness, a little longing when we are young, a little futile striving for work, a little passionate striving for room for the exercise of her powers – and then we go with the drove. A woman must march with her regiment. In the end she must be trodden down or go with it.' In her girls' school she had not learned what she had expected. 'I have discovered that of all cursed places under the sun, where the hungriest soul can hardly pick up a few grains of knowledge, a girls' boarding school is the worst. They are called finishing schools and the name tells accurately what they are . . .' Olive Schreiner has been described as 'a suffragette before there were any.'

Waldo and Lyndall drive together over the veld. They sit on a kopje and talk. He takes her to a Boer dance. Then she goes away. Gregory Rose feels the first real emotion of his life: he goes in search of her, wants nothing but to serve her. Waldo leaves in search of wider experience. Em stays and suffers. Lyndall has become pregnant by a 'stranger, his tall slight figure reposing in the broken armchair, his keen blue eyes studying the fire from beneath delicately pencilled drooping eyelids. One white hand plays with a heavy flaxen mustache.' This figure, or a similar one, appears and reappears through Olive Schreiner's work. He is charged with the high tension of conflict, a man found overwhelmingly sexually attractive, but contemptibly wanting by a woman who demands moral and intellectual companionship, as well as physical, from her lover The stranger wants to marry Lyndall. She will not: it will put her in his power, and he only decided to marry her when he

realized that she might not want to. But she agrees to stay
with him, unmarried, for the sake of the child. They travel
around the Cape, but some quarrel occurs. She is left alone
and ill. Gregory Rose tracks her down to a country hotel. She
needs a nurse. He dresses himself in women's clothes and
looks after her. The baby dies soon after it is born. She dies
too. Waldo returns to the farm after eighteen months of every
sort of degrading labour. He has learned that: 'You may work
and work and work until you are only a body and not a soul.'
Gregory returns with the news of Lyndall's death. He will
marry Em because Lyndall has told him to. Em says: 'Why is
it always so, Waldo, always so? We long for things and long
for them and pray for them. Then at last, too late, when we
don't want them any more, when all the sweetness is taken
out of them, then they come.'

Waldo goes off to sit in the sunshine – and dies.

Lyndall is dead. Waldo is dead. The saintly old man is
dead.

Gregory Rose lives to carry on the farm with gentle
uncomplaining Em who, Lyndall says, 'is so much better than
me that there is more goodness in her little finger than in my
whole body.' Tant' Sannie, remarried, flourishes with her
new husband.

Well, that's the story. Parts are well done by the conventional yardstick: the scenes of rural Boer life; the
dance, the scene where the young man comes in 'his hopeless
resignation' to court Tant' Sannie; Tant' Sannie coming to
visit with her new baby; Tant' Sannie on the joys of marriage;
Tant' Sannie on progress: 'Not that I believe in this new plan
of putting soda into the pot. If the dear Father had meant
soda to be put into soap, what would He have made
milkbushes for, and stuck them all over the veld, as thick as
lambs in lambing season.' This woman, as near animal as
they come, is written with love and with humour – a

triumph. Em, too, the maiden dreaming of motherhood: 'I always come to watch the milking. That red cow with the short horns is bringing up the calf of the white cow that died. She loves it so – just as if it were her own. It is so nice to see her lick its little ears. Just look!' Now, these are characters that could have appeared in any good novel called *Scenes from the Karroo, 18–*. It did not take Olive Schreiner to create them. The novel's greatness lies precisely in where it breaks from 'lifelike' characters, and an easily recognizable probability.

There is the question of Bonaparte Blenkins, the charlatan. Later Olive said she was sorry that she had given him no real humanity, made him two-dimensional. But her first instinct was right. Evil is not personified in this book – neither is goodness. Human beings are small things in the grip of gigantic forces. They cry out and fight and struggle to understand the incomprehensible, which is beyond good and evil. Had Bonaparte been given depth and weight, we would have had to ask questions about the saintliness of the old German, Bonaparte's counterweight, whom he has to destroy. He is saintly: but very silly. And Bonaparte is wicked – and silly. Not damaging? Indeed, yes: his persecution of the old German, his treatment of Waldo, the brutal beating he gave him, scarred Waldo, and taught him his helplessness; taught Lyndall her helplessness, and enforced her determination to free herself. But he was stupid, undid himself – and ran away. Wickedness is arbitrary, almost grotesque. And innocent childlike goodness is impotent. But – does it matter all that much? The sun burns down over the Karroo; the pitilessly indifferent stars wheel and deploy; and two young creatures look up at the skies where they see their unimportance written, and ask questions, can find no answers – and suffer most frightfully.

Lyndall and Waldo: Olive said that in these two she had put herself. They share a soul; and when Lyndall dies, Waldo has to die. But it is Waldo who is the heart of the book, a ragged, sullen, clumsy farm boy, all inarticulate hunger – not for education, like Lyndall, but for the unknown. And it is to Waldo that Olive gave the chapter that is the core, not only of this novel, but of all her work. It is called 'Waldo's stranger,' and in it a man travelling through the Cape stops to rest on the farm for an hour. Waldo has carved a piece of wood. 'It was by no means lovely. The men and birds were almost grotesque in their laboured resemblance to nature, and bore signs of patient thought. The stranger turns the thing over on his knee . . .' and offers to buy it for £5. Waldo, whom he sees as 'a hind' says no: it is for his father's grave. The visitor is touched, presses the boy to talk, and finally, understanding his need, puts what Waldo has carved on the stick into a story. This is the legend of The Hunter. A version, or germ, of this tale appears in Attar's Parliament of the Birds. 'An astonishing thing! The first manifestation of the Simurgh' (God or what you will) 'took place in China in the middle of the night. One of his feathers fell on China and his reputation filled the world. Everyone made a picture of this feather, and from it formed his own system of ideas, and so fell into a turmoil. This feature is still in the picture gallery of that country: hence the saying: "Seek knowledge, even as far as China." But for his manifestation there would not have been so much noise in the world concerning this mysterious Being. This sign of his existence is a token of his glory. All souls carry an impression of the image of his feather. Since the description of it has neither head nor tail, beginning nor end, it is not necessary to say more about it. Now, any of you who are for this road, prepare yourself and put your feet on the Way.' The Hunter of the Stranger's tale has tried all his life to climb the mountains whose summits hold the Truth, cutting steps in the rock so that he, and others after him, can climb. He lies dying, alone. Long ago he has shed the childish arrogance that let him believe he could find Truth: what matters is that he has spent his life trying. Then: 'Slowly from the white sky above, through the still air, came something falling, falling, falling. Softly it fluttered down and dropped on to the breast of the dying man. He felt it with his hands. It was a feather. He died holding it.' What Olive makes of this tale is both all her own, and from that region of the human mind called Anon.

Lyndall, too, is visited by a stranger, who gave her, at just the time she needed that book, a book. In Olive's own life it was Spencer's First Principles, and she read it, sleepless, for the three days she was able to keep it. To us, the battle for education having been won, at least for this time and for the fortunate of the world, knowledge as it emerges filtered through school and university is perhaps not as covetable as what Olive Schreiner was able to make of books, by herself, using her own instinct to find what she needed. But Lyndall's passion for an education would be understood now by an African boy (or girl) who wants an education so badly that he will walk or bicycle ten, fifteen miles, from a mud hut, or a bunk in a shed in a shanty-town shared with half dozen others, to a day's hard labour; walk or cycle back; and then walk, bicycle, as many miles in another direction to sit up till midnight in an ill-equipped classroom run by a half-equipped teacher, so as to learn to read, write, and do arithmetic. For which 'education' he will pay, or his parents will, money he needs for food and clothes. There are millions of them in Africa. To such people books, learning, are a key to freedom – as they are to Lyndall, who, when she got them, discovered their limits.

But Waldo wanted a different kind of knowledge, and that is what he was given by his stranger, to whom he says: 'All my life I have longed to see you.' He was thinking: Ah, that man who believed nothing, hoped nothing, felt nothing: *how he loved him*. And, when the stranger was gone, he stooped and kissed passionately a footprint in the sand.

Lyndall has given her name to dozens of little South African girls: the beautiful young woman who chooses to die alone rather than marry a man she cannot respect. Lyndall is that projection of a novelist created as a means of psychic self-preservation. Olive, at that time, was very much alone. If not estranged from her family, she could not get from it the moral support she so badly needed She was very young. She was ill: was to be ill all her life. She had been through violent religious conflicts that had left her drained, exhausted. She had been in love with, possibly jilted by, a man who found her socially inadequate, and morally and mentally his superior – or so the evidence suggests. That Olive should have needed Lyndall is not surprising: she had to love Lyndall, and stand by her, and protect her – and explain her; for Lyndall was the first of her kind in fiction. Of her we can say: that kind of embattled woman was the product of that kind of society, where women had a hard time of it. But Waldo is the truth of Lyndall, and he is timeless.

Women novelists' men . . . Male novelists' women can be as instructive, particularly in their archetypal state, like Haggard's *She* – as the psychologists have pointed out. This 'she' is best studied in bad novels, for in good novels she is a human being. And so with women writers' men; the most useful exemplars we have being Rochester and Heathcliff. They are the unregenerate strong man, the unfulfilled hero. In the psyche of men, is the goddess, 'she.' In women, the hero; but it is as if women, looking for strength, the hero, the strong wise man who embodies humanity's struggle upwards, and not finding him, may take instead his failed brother, who at least has had potentiality; rather than a nothing-man who has never aimed at anything. Lyndall's lover, with his flaxen moustaches and his heavy eyelids; the rest of the attractive men who capture Olive Schreiner's heroines against their will – they are nothing-men, put there to be despised. But the hero, the strong man who challenges destiny: well, his place is of course with 'she' – in legend, myth, and magic. He cannot exist, in his pure form, in the novel, that struggling and impure art. He is out of place there, as 'she' is. You find her, him, only in romantic or second-rate novels. But Waldo is the first appearance in women's writing of the true hero, in a form appropriate to the novel; here a kind of Caliban who mysteriously embodies Prospero's spirit, or Faust's.

Waldo is the son of the old German, Otto, who is a portrait of Olive's father.

To the creation of a woman novelist seem to go certain psychological ingredients; at least, often enough to make it interesting. One of them, a balance between father and mother where the practicality, the ordinary sense, cleverness, and worldly ambition is on the side of the mother; and the father's life is so weighted with dreams and ideas and imaginings that their joint life gets lost in what looks like a hopeless muddle and failure, but which holds a potentiality for something that must be recognized as better, on a different level, than what ordinary sense or cleverness can begin to conceive.

Olive's mother was the daughter of a minister of religion destined for a good middle-class marriage. She met Gottlob Schreiner at a missionary meeting. He was a student, the son of a German shoemaker, in a family of peasants and preachers. At the wedding the minister tore the trimmings off Rebecca's hat, as unsuitable for the wife of a missionary. They went off together to the Cape, in a mood of high evangelical fervour, to convert the heathen. Gottlob never lost his sense of mission, but his wife later declared it was all 'claptrap and nonsense.' She tried to preserve some intellectual life, and the respectable standards of her upbringing, in isolation and in poverty, while he loved and idealized her as a being quite above him. She was educated, beautiful, clever – and frustrated. Olive, the sixth child, experienced her as cold and unloving. 'My mother has never been a mother to me. I have had no mother. She is a brilliant, wonderful little woman, all intellect and genius. The relation between us is a very curious one . . . she seems to me like a favourite brilliant child of mine.' Olive was solitary, 'queer,' and fanciful in a way all the family found uncomfortable. She grew up on poor mission stations, in close relationship with the wild untenanted landscape of the Cape. This saved her: according to modern ideas, she was brutally treated; but she escaped to the rocks, the bushes, the sun, the stars. *Undine* describes her childhood. From the time she was a baby playing with dolls, she was tormented by God, by hell, by redemption – she was reading the Bible before she read anything – and by her own passionate uncompromising temperament, and the conscience that was the product of her Lutheran, Wesleyan, heritage. In crises of misery over God, there could be no comfort in her family: she was locked up, punished. She was beaten: her worst was from her mother, who gave her fifty strokes on her bare body with a bunch of quince rods. This was for using a crude Dutch expression: she said 'Ach!' Rebecca and her fight for respectability emerges, in this incident, as if into a spotlight. Olive was never able to forget this experience. To read *Undine* is painful even now, not so much for the punishings and the beatings, but because of her hunger for love, for understanding, and the mental anguish that she suffered for years. Lying awake at night she listened to the clock tick: every tick meant souls were being sent to hell by an unforgiving God. She cried out to be given some burden or sacrifice so that even one soul might be spared because of her. She staged sacrifices like Abraham, putting a mutton chop saved from dinner onto a rock in the midday sun, and waiting for the fire to come from heaven – for she had as much faith as Abraham. But nothing happened, God was indifferent to her. She got up at night to read the Bible by moonlight, to find some words that might comfort her, and found: 'Strive to enter in at the strait gate, for many, I say unto you, shall seek to enter in and shall not be able.' She flung the Bible across the room and wept, and stared at the stars out of the window, and was tormented by eternity and the littleness of human beings on their earth. She lost her faith, and knew that she was wicked, and was damned, but preferred the expectation of hell and rejection by God than to accept God's injustice, which made some souls elect from the beginning of time, and others inevitably damned. Many Victorians, fighting a narrow and bigoted religion, lost their reputations, their jobs, sometimes their reason: their conflicts are described in plentiful memoirs from that time. But this frightful battle was fought out in a small girl, who had no one to help her. When still a girl she became 'a freethinker' and remained one, always contemptuous of conventional religion. Asked for help, much later, by a parson threatened with loss of faith, she wrote: 'If I must put it into words, I would say, the Universe is One, and It lives; or, if you would put it into older phraseology, There is NOTHING but God.' Sympathetic but not very insightful contemporaries defended her by saying she was a religious woman who did not believe in God. She said of herself that she had that deep faith that took the form of a lifelong battle with God, and which took for granted she would be forgiven: which is not the same thing at all. But to her, our almost casual rejection of God, an indifferent irreligiousness, would have been impossible.

The Victorians who fought that battle carried their free-thinking, their agnosticism, their atheism, like flags of faith in the free spirit of man. The question she makes us ask, as do all the great ones of the past, is: If she were alive now, what battle would she be fighting? The freedoms she fought for, we take for granted. Because of people like her. We tend to forget that. She never did; was searching literature and history for allies even as a child; and before she was twenty had read Darwin and Spencer, Montaigne, Goethe, Carlyle, Gibbon, Locke, and Lecky; J. S. Mill, Shakespeare, Ruskin, and Schiller. And had made amateur attempts, her mother aiding, at medicine and biology and anatomy. For poor Rebecca had once dreamed of studying medicine.

The family disintegrated in poverty, Gottlob was irremediably incompetent, and gave away what he possessed, often to rogues. He died, and the mother, extraordinarily, became a Roman Catholic, though according to the chapel creed, 'one of the three grand crimes was to believe in the possible salvation of a Roman Catholic.' Some of the children found it a crime; but not Olive, who continued to love her mother with that kind of love that is all a hopeful need. It was rewarded. As a woman she wrote, with deep emotion, how one night she woke to find her mother crying in her bed. Rebecca had read something Olive had written and was saying: 'Oh, my child, my wonderful beautiful child. Am I really your mother ? Have I really given birth to a human being who could write like that? You could never have written this if you had not been thinking of your own childhood. Forgive me, please.'

At nineteen Olive became a governess, and taught for seven years in the families of Boer farmers. Here she learned 'to love and admire the Boer.' In one of her places her room was mud-floored, and when it rained she had to put up an umbrella, because the roof leaked. The furniture was a bed and a box for her clothes. There was no looking-glass, not even a basin: she washed in the stream that ran past her door. But she was content here, moved for health reasons: her asthma began at this time. In these years she wrote drafts of *Undine*, *From Man to Man*, and completed *The Story of an African Farm*. Because of 'the autobiographical element' she had affection for *Undine*, but she asked for it to be destroyed. She was right: it is an undigested, mental book, in parts not far away from the pathetic Victorian novel at its worst. Other people knew better, and it was published. *From Man to Man* she cared for, and worked on it all her life. But while it is full of plums, that fusing that makes a work of art never took place. What, then, fused the *Farm*? Possibly the unhappy love affair. We do not know. She did not care for these emotions to be made public, and we should respect that. Though certainly they scarred her, and she said so; but for her, pain was a teacher, and painful experience necessary for growth.

After she became a literary figure in London, it is harder to see her clearly. She appears in the reminiscences of other people, as in a series of posed photographs. 'Distinctly pretty with large dark eyes and black hair and the little square, strong figure.' That was Frank Harris. And Havelock Ellis on their first meeting: '. . . the short sturdy, vigorous body in loose shapeless clothes, sitting on the couch, with the hands spread on her thighs and, above, the beautiful head with the large dark eyes, at once so expressive and so observant.'

Her first desire to meet people was soon swallowed in the necessity for privacy: she found she had no time to write or to study. She seems always to be in flight – away from people, and towards some place where at last she could feel well. There are letters; but letters, as I think biographers tend to forget, are written to people, and reflect those people, or the phase of a relationship, as much as they do the writer.

Letters to Havelock Ellis are best: she called him her other self, her brother; and over the decades they were in correspondence there is maintained the steady note of intellectual sympathy, even when in emotional stress with each other. They might have married. He was more explicit about his side than she about hers: she did not love him enough, he said. But both were contradictory about each other, as they were bound to be in a friendship that lasted till she died and survived their marriages to other people. Her letters describe her conflicts over marriage. 'I can't marry, Henry, I can't. And some awful power seems to be drawing me on. I think I shall go mad. I couldn't. I *must* be free you know, I *must* be free . . .' 'Oh Henry, when passion enters a relationship it does spoil the holy sweetness. But perhaps those people are right who say no such thing as friendship is possible between man and woman, though I can't bear to think so.' 'The lesson of the last 5 years has been that there is no such thing as friendship, just as the lesson of the two before was that there is no such thing as sex-love, only sex-selfishness.' 'Please love me. I wish I could believe anything was real . . .' 'Life would be so perfect, so beautiful, so divine, but I think I'm reaching a kind of Nirvana. I can't feel much personally, nor desire much for myself . . . *Self* seems to be dead in me. Other people want to kill self, but I want so to wake mine to life again, but it won't wake. You know I didn't kill myself two years ago, but I really died then . . .' 'Sweet brother soul, don't feel far from me. I too am going through a very dark and bitter moment of my life . . .' '. . . for so many years I have longed to meet a mind that should understand me, that should take away from the loneliness of my life. Now I have found it . . .' 'In that you are myself, I love you, and am near to you, but in that you are a man I am afraid of you, I shrink from you.'

I think all this is simpler than it sounds. The 'anguish and

ecstasy' of her childhood had burned her out emotionally
before childhood had properly ended. She was tranquil – but
dead. She was writing about such states before she was out
of her teens, a kind of dark night of the emotions where she
felt neither love, nor hate, nor hope, and would have
welcomed even pain. Then she fell in love, came to life in
hopes for the marriage that did not happen, and was again
in the cold hell of no-feeling. Havelock Ellis could not free
her from it, but later her husband did. Her letters to Ellis
show the evasiveness of a woman who is fond of a man she
does not find sexually compelling. She needed him, loved
him; but could not respond as he wanted – and as she
wanted.

She was in Europe, mostly England, for almost a decade.
Through a fog of illness: asthma, heart trouble, neuralgia,
which she knew to be what we call psychosomatic, though
knowing it did not help her; through the confusion of her
emotional conflict; we can watch the growth of another side
of Olive Schreiner. The social reformer was becoming a
socialist. She met, became friends with, the socialists:
Eleanor Marx was an intimate. And the feminist learned that
what had been, in her girlhood, a solitary personal
conviction, considered eccentric, was what the best men and
women of her time were studying. It was called The Woman
Question. Always practical, always at the roots of any
problem, she was helping poor women, prostitutes, women
in every kind of trouble. She started work on a 'big scientific
work' on sex, which she discussed with Havelock Ellis. It
never saw the light; was destroyed in the Boer War. A pity;
no one else could have written it so well, and no one can
write it now. For sex changes, like everything else, must be
part of a climate. Between that time, such a short time ago,
and ourselves is such a gulf of experience that it is hard to
imagine ourselves in an air where so much was twisted,

dark, murky. For instance, part of her suffering was due to celibacy: she said it herself. But: 'I would so much like to have a child, but I couldn't bear to be married; neither could I bear any relationship that was not absolutely open to the world – so I could never have one.' This was written at a time she was being asked to leave lodgings by landladies who considered her immoral because she had single men and 'unrespectable' women visiting her. She continued to act as she believed she had the right to act; yet she was a woman so sensitive to notice she hated even to eat in public. There is one large lesson we can still learn from the battle over 'the woman question.' It is that a change in physical relations and conditions changes mental and emotional states beyond what even the most revolutionary of reformers can begin to foresee. Even Olive, considered wildly visionary about the future of women, was far from seeing how much that was considered innate, inherent, could disappear and how fast. None of them ever seemed far from a micro-climate of semi-invalidism. Take what used to be called 'the change of life,' which even our mothers faced and suffered like a dreaded illness. For most women now it doesn't exist, and for many it happens without the aid of drugs. Less than a hundred years has done it. How? Why? The book that was destroyed could have helped with these and with other questions that ought to be asked. But there is a generation of girls enjoying liberties won for them by women like Olive Schreiner and looking back with what seems to be patronage, amusement. It is really a shudder of terror at what they've escaped from – and it stops them thinking.

It was mostly South Africa's sun, which might help her health, that took her back there in 1889. She was now a public figure; and she took a stand on 'The Native Question' and on Rhodes' acquisition of what became Southern Rhodesia. At first she admired Rhodes, who always admired her. She became his enemy over his doubledealing in the Jameson Raid; and wrote a novel called *Trooper Peter Halkett of Mashonaland*, which was good enough for its purpose: an effort to arouse public indignation. It did. But it didn't stop Rhodes from annexing Mashonaland. She continued to protest and to warn while the bases of modern South Africa and Rhodesia were being well and truly laid. If Africans were not admitted now, she said, into the fellowship of civilization, it would soon be too late; and the future would be all bloodshed and misery. She was prophetic about this, as about so much else; and emotionally clear in a way that she must have found hard to achieve. It is difficult enough now for a white person brought up in white-dominated Africa to free himself, herself, from a prejudice that starts when, from the moment you see anything, you see Africans as inferiors. The child Olive was taught to despise 'kaffirs' and 'niggers.' Parts of *Undine* show an ignorance and prejudice that is now shocking. She was also taught to despise the Dutch. When she was four, a small Boer girl gave her some sugar. She accepted, 'not liking to refuse,' but dropped it afterwards, for one did not eat anything that had been held in the hand of a Boer child. She also had conventionally prejudiced ideas about Jews, though there is a possibility she was part Jewish. All this she had to fight in herself, to change, in order to become the champion of racial tolerance. Nor was she that kind of liberal that South Africa still produces, the paternalist who believes that the kindly-master-to-grateful-servant relationship is the only one possible, since it is the only one he has ever seen. Olive, a real revolutionary, knew that the dispossessed must always work for, and win, their own rights, their own freedom; because it is in the fighting, the working, that they grow and develop and learn their measure. She expressed this idea particularly well in her writing about women.

Afterword to The Story of an African Farm

When she was nearly forty, this woman who said she could not marry married a South African farmer, rather younger than herself. There were times of great happiness, though the marriage was difficult, as it was bound to be. The much-longed-for child died, and particularly cruelly; it choked in its sleep the night after it was born. Her grief turned her again towards the dark, weakened her, and, it seems, the marriage which, however, continued to be buoyed by their common love for South Africa and by their sympathy over political questions. In the Boer War she championed the Boers against her own countrymen, by whom she was reviled. She loved England. She loved the Boers. She suffered acutely, but she kept her good judgement, as her book 'An English South African's View of the Situation' shows. It throws light even now, for the violent emotionalism of the time did not prevent her from holding on to the essentials: that it was the black people who would shape the future; and that in South Africa any conflicts were (and are) bound to be over who owns the gold, the diamonds, the minerals. In the bitter aftermath of the war she worked for an alliance between British and Dutch that would include the black people. These views were as unpopular then as they are now: but now she would be in exile or in prison. Her husband always supported her, though some sympathies were wearing thin. He had made sacrifices for the marriage. The farm he loved (so did she) was given up: her health was bad there. He had made another profession for himself, but there were money shortages; and he complained that he had counted on her earning money through books that in fact she did not get written. Above all, her health grew worse. She spent nights without sleep, walking around the house, talking to herself, fighting for breath. The drugs she took affected her badly. Her behaviour, always 'free,' was increasingly unconventional, and Cronwright was upset by it. She had never cared about her dress. At this time she is described as dowdy, unimpressive, with none of her old fire and brilliance – until she stands up to address a meeting, when she is electrifying. She is described as the sort of woman who in an older society would have been made the prophetess of a tribe. In short, being married to her must have been extremely uncomfortable; and the older she grew, the less important became the small everyday things where a marriage has to live. She suffered, increasingly, from the states of mind we label, in one of our sterilizing, nullifying words, 'depressions.' She also had deeper, more frequent glimpses into states of insight and ecstatic oneness that were for her the meaning of life.

In some ways, she narrowed; was finding far too many things, and people, and kinds of writing 'coarse' or 'crude.' She sounded, sometimes, like a prissy maiden aunt. Women as they get older seem prone to this: witness Virginia Woolf on James Joyce. I think it is because women find it hard to be public. If it is not against our deepest nature, for what our deepest nature is seems a matter of doubt when things change so fast, it is certain that public women attract a certain kind of spite, a bitchiness, from both men and women. Learning not to care about this can create a reactive overemphasis: 'You say I am unfeminine: look at my traditional female moral attitudes!' Olive earned her share of spite; and she continued over-sensitive, an unfortunate trait for someone always in the public eye and always fighting on the unpopular side. She never grew a most essential protective skin: somewhere in her was the young woman who, like Charlotte Brontë, had chosen to be a young man, 'Ralph Iron,' rather than expose herself to criticism, and this at a time when she was known as a feminist. But these are small faults in a big woman whose essential self was generous and wide, whose scope was always enlarging, and who continued to work for women. Cronwright does not seem to have been as sympathetic over this as over her other crusades. At least, there is a note of tetchiness here. But he did support and help her; and in 1911 she published *Woman and Labour*, which had an immediate and extraordinary influence, became a kind of bible for the feminists But, like all her social writing, it goes much deeper than the temporary conditions it describes.

The First World War interrupted the suffragettes' and Olive's work for women; Olive's work for South Africa – and for peace. She was a pacifist. She was in England during the war. Her husband stayed in South Africa. These years must have been bad ones for her. Most of the socialists and suffragettes who were her natural allies had swung into support of the war. Many of her oldest friends found her position unsympathetic. She hated all wars, for any reason, and this one seemed to her particularly wrong. The jingoist nationalism of the time was loathsome to her. She remained for the most part quiet and alone – when she was not being turned out of lodgings and reported to the police because of her German name. In 1917 she saluted the birth of communist Russia among a most remarkable assortment of people, in The 1917 Club: Ramsey Macdonald, Oswald Mosley, Bertrand Russell, E. M. Forster, H. W. Nevinson. But she had said for years that the future lay with Russia and with America: a view that seemed absurd. When the war ended, her husband did not recognize the old woman who answered the door to him. She asked him to go back to the Cape with her. But she sailed alone, seen off by him and by Havelock Ellis. She was very ill. Soon afterwards she died alone in a hotel in the Cape.

What is left of this wonderful woman is *The Story of an African Farm*. The great influence she had is hidden from us in the events she helped to shape. It is the right time for this book to be republished. There is an atmosphere that is sympathetic to it, particularly among young people. It makes me very happy to introduce Olive Schreiner to a fresh generation of readers because:

> It seems to me more and more that the only thing that really matters in life is not wealth or poverty, pleasure or hardship, but the nature of the human beings with whom one is thrown into contact, and one's relation with them.

Allah Be Praised

Malcolm X's autobiography is not an autobiography. A ghost, Alex Haley, made this book – most of it approved by Malcolm X before he died – from speeches, articles, notes of interviews. Against difficulties. Haley is a Negro, but was first regarded by Malcolm X as 'a white man's tool sent to spy.' 'I trust you 70 per cent' was his way of announcing won confidence. Then, the Black Muslim section was done before the break, while Malcolm X was passionately identified with the movement and its leader, Elijah Muhammad. As any politician would, he glossed over the internal difficulties to which he was not deliberately blinding himself. Nor, after the break, could his loyalty to the Negro struggle allow him damaging admissions. So if you want facts about membership, hidden allegiances, military organization and plans, this book is worthless. Worse: Malcolm X's viewpoint about himself and his ideas shifted during the writing of it. Which brings up again the point recently raised by Truman Capote and his murderers – a relationship between reporter and subject which is bound to be suspicious, resistant, hostile, then overconfiding. Malcolm X was alone, trusted no one, not even his wife, was paranoiac. Like the hero of *Catch-22*, classified as paranoid for believing – a soldier in World War II – that people wanted to kill him.

Haley got nowhere until he carefully depth-bombed: 'I wonder if you'd tell me something about your mother.' 'After that night he never hesitated to tell me the most intimate details of his personal life.' 'It made me face something about myself,' said Malcolm X – and face himself he did, uncovering areas blocked off through misery, drugs, guilt, hate. Malcolm X was not by nature gifted with insight into himself. Learning it came hard. About what he learned he was immediately honest, with the kind of frankness which comes easiest to those who are able to see their lives impersonally, as representative of forces larger than themselves – in his case, the Negro struggle for freedom. His sharply shifting viewpoints about his past would have made this book an unsatisfactory patchwork even if it hadn't used the hypnotic rhetoric of the speeches, the provocative over-simplifications of the polemical writing, as if these were Malcolm X's considered voice. Much better to have had this straight biography from the shrewd and compassionate Haley. *But*, should we really welcome books like these, where a man in such a prison is opened in trust for the first time to a reporter doing a job?

Malcolm X's father preached God and was an active follower of Garvey, who taught that Negroes must return to Africa since they could never achieve freedom in America. When Malcolm X's mother was pregnant with him, horsed and hooded Ku Klux Klansmen surrounded the house one night, brandishing guns and threats. His mother fended them off. When Malcolm X was four, the house was burned over the family's heads by two white men. The police did not catch the white men, but harassed the father about the gun he had used to try to defend himself. Malcolm's father had seen four of his six brothers die by violence, one by lynching. He was very black. Malcolm's mother was West Indian, her father a white man.

His father favoured Malcolm as the lightest child – he had red hair, was almost white – but the mother whipped him

186

extra. It was a fighting marriage: she was educated and patronized her rougher husband. The family lived in poverty, mostly on prayer-meeting collections. The small boy admired his father because he was 'tough and scared the white folks to death.' When the child was six the father was murdered by white men. The mother tried to keep eight children on charring jobs, which she lost when it was found she was the agitator's widow. She was proud, fought against charity, had to take it. The children were starving. Welfare people gave food, and patronage, which was bitterly resented. The children watched her slow breakup: she was committed to a mental hospital and they were boarded out. Malcolm was twelve. An intransigent child, he was sent to reform school. There, for once, he struck it lucky with the people who ran it, though he noted they would talk about 'niggers' in front of him, and 'it never dawned on them I wasn't a pet but a human being.' He was bright, worked hard, was elected class president. But his only period of social conformity ended when, asked by the white teacher what he planned for his future, he replied 'to be a lawyer' – which he was obviously born for – and was told that as a Negro he must be realistic and settle for carpentry. It should be noted that this was not in the South, but near Detroit, in 1940. He went to Boston to stay with his formidable sister Ella, who planned respectability for him. He was sixteen. Within a year he was a criminal in Harlem, accepted by a fraternity that sounds as exclusive as a crafts union, because of his wits and courage. Also he had a status symbol, an upper-class white girl who was at his disposal for five years, whom he fleeced of money, and despised. He was revenging himself on the white race through sex. His voice, like Baldwin's, is theatrically accusing – but as long as there are white people who enjoy being trounced for their total inferiority, particularly sexual, I suppose we'll have to listen to it. He traded in drugs, liquor, gambling, sex; thieved, pimped – survived. These chapters should be required reading for our persistent sentimentalists about black slums. This is what it is really like to live on one's wits in Harlem: and presumably in any black ghetto in America. (And in South Africa, be it noted.) At last, demoralized by cocaine, opium, hashish, liquor, he was caught, his white mistress and another white woman with him. Because there were white women involved, the sentences were heavy for a first offence.

He was then twenty-one, and he served seven years. A fellow prisoner called Bimbi told him to use the prison correspondence courses and library. He impressed Malcolm X as 'the first man I'd known who commanded total respect – with his words.' Painfully, he rehabilitated himself by copying out the dictionary, word by word; learned Latin and grammar; read systematically. Still in prison, he heard of the Black Muslims and suffered a conversion, which he compares with St Paul's, to the 'true knowledge.' This truth was brought to America by a prophet as great as Jesus or Mohammed, called Mr Wallace D. Fard, from whom Elijah Muhammad learned historical facts hitherto concealed by the white man from the Negro. It seems that 6,000 years ago a mad scientist (in defiance of God and to punish the world) created the white race out of the black race, which is genetically the true one. The white man is the devil of the Bible and has deliberately corrupted the black man through slavery and Christian brainwashing. The only hope for the black man is total separation from the white, who is evil beyond redemption. Something like apartheid: the Black Muslim creed is the mirror image of the white racialist one. Malcolm X came out of prison into the arms of Elijah Muhammad, whom he believed to be an aspect of Allah, the black man's God. He had turned into his own opposite, embracing puritanism with all the fervour of his nature. The

Nation of Islam don't smoke or drink; observe strict dietary laws; every hour of the day is regulated by religious observance; their women wear a uniform like a nun's dress; the penalties for not being chaste and monogamous are expulsion and ostracism.

Whereas Malcolm X the Harlem hustler had gloried in the sexual power-game of the race war's shadowlands, chalking up every white man or woman attracted by black flesh as evidence of the white man's corruption, now he preached against sex like a latter-day Calvin so that the Brotherhood were always complaining to the leader that he was anti-woman. Then he married, found happiness, and was able to admit: 'I guess by now I will say I love Betty.' Clearly, he loved her very much, even if he was able to trust her only 75 per cent.

As for Elijah Muhammad, a man worshipped as God by a small, manageable sect, he was embarrassed by his fanatical lieutenant, a brilliant organizer, polemicist, politician, who wanted nothing less than the total conversion of all the Negroes in the United States. In the twelve years Malcolm X was a Minister, he transformed the black Muslims into an efficient, growing, internationally known organisation which had America hopping – and all this in the name of his leader, to whom, and to Allah, he gave the credit. Cassius Clay was a recruit and, although a close friend of Malcolm's, he remained after the break. Then Elijah Muhummad was publicly faced with two paternity suits by ex-secretaries. Trying to save his world from crashing, Malcolm X took precedents from the Bible to his leader, who said:

Son, you always had such a good understanding of prophecy and spiritual things. I'm David, who took another man's wife. You read about Noah who got drunk – that's me. You read about Lot, who went and laid up his own daughters. I have to fulfil all these things.

Malcolm X was unable to turn his back on Muhammad, but Muhammad had decided to get rid of Malcolm X Probably by murder: Malcolm X thought so – he had himself trained the young men in the military arts and had said, 'I know what they are capable of.' But he had always known he would die by violence and 'tried to be ready for it.' Meanwhile he went to Mecca on pilgrimage, and learned that what he had been preaching as 'Islam' had little to do with the real Islam. Race hatred, for instance, was no part of it. This section of the book, in which he is entertained by Islamic and nationalist leaders in the Middle East and in Africa, reads embarrassingly like Jennifer's Diary – as painful as the reminiscences of African nationalist leaders who, taken to the MRA headquarters in Caux, may return converted because 'they treated me like a human being.' But they seldom stay converted.

Malcolm X came home with a new name, El-Hajj Malik El Shabbaz (his 'X' had 'replaced the white slavemaster name of "Little," which some blue-eyed devil named Little had imposed upon my paternal forebears'). He came home, too, with considerably modified ideas. With his usual courage he said so: he was expecting assassination daily. His tactical sense was put to the service of new outlooks. If he had lived, his version of 'The Nation of Islam' would probably have manoeuvred usefully in conjunction with the moderate movements formerly described by him as 'Uncle Tom': as a Black Muslim lieutenant, he had chafed because Muhammad would not allow collaboration. He was murdered in 1965 while addressing a meeting in New York.

The Black Muslim sect remains: so does Elijah Muhammad. Its value – apart from its work among ex-prisoners, junkies, prostitutes – has been largely propagandist. The moderate movements, 'the sit-downs, sit-ins and teach-ins,' have achieved more in practical terms. If, as the

Allah Be Praised

Black Muslims believed, the devil white man can be terrified by threats of raw violence into parting with his privileges, then Los Angeles would be a better place for their race riots. I gather this is not the case. But what a pity he is dead. He was a most gifted man, and we don't know what he might have become.

In the World, Not of It

That East must ever be East and West must be West is not a belief which is subscribed to by Sufis, who claim that Sufism, in its reality, not necessarily under the name, is continuously in operation in every culture. Sometimes invisible, it is at times offered as openly as goods in a supermarket. When this happens, it is expected by them that there will be hostility from those academics who have made orientalism their property, and sometimes from literary or other authoritarian bodies. During well over 1,000 years of connected literary and psychological tradition, embracing Spain, North Africa, Central Asia, and the Middle East, they have almost invariably clashed with narrow thinkers. Often the struggle between Sufis and the 'establishments' looks unpleasantly like what happened when the Nazis took a stand against something. Some past patterns are unfamiliar to us; others can still be instructive, for in one form or another they repeat themselves.

Hallaj was dismembered in Baghdad, A.D. 922, for blasphemy. The evidence against him included the dread indictment that he was the grandson of a Zoroastrian, and that he was 'ignorant of the Koran and its ancillary sciences of juris-prudence, traditions, etc. and of poetry and Arabic philology'.[1] Searches of the houses of some of

1. E. G. Browne *Literary History of Persia* (Cambridge: Cambridge University Press, 1928 [1964 edition]).

193

his followers showed that they actually possessed books inscribed in gold on Chinese paper. In case you didn't know it, this was taken to suggest that the writings must be heretical, since Manichees used gold ink and Chinese paper.

Suhrawardi was killed in 1191, the charge including 'atheism, heresy, and believing in ancient philosophers.'

Ibn El Arabi of Spain was hauled before an inquisition of scholars in the twelfth century, for immodesty in pretending that love poetry could be spiritual, when it was pornographic.

Sarmad was executed in India in 1563 for exposing his body; he was alleged to be a Jew or of Jewish origin.

Jalaluddin Rumi was accused of publishing trivial folk tales in the guise of spiritual writings.

There were sometimes difficulties in attacking the Sufis, once they had established a name for literature, or could not be shown to be vicious. One such case is the frame-up of Nasimi. Unable to fault Nasimi in argument, certain scholars sent him a pair of shoes as a gift, from another country. Into the sole they had sewn a chapter from the Koran. Then they sent word to the Governor of Aleppo that Nasimi was defiling the Koran. The Governor had his shoe slit open. On the production of the paper Nasimi made no answer to the charger, knowing that he was going to be killed. He was flayed alive, reciting verses.

The charges are always the same. The academic scholars persecute, claim apostasy, ignorance, dubious parentage, desire for power over the people, danger to public order, self-advertisement and the circulation of spurious, superficial, or irresponsible literature. But in spite of these accusations, in spite of persecution often followed by judicial murder, the Sufi teachers subsequently became major spiritual authorities to the Islamic world. Most of these Sufis were literary men, and all were marked by their inability to accept the dogmas of their current 'establishments.' Once safely dead, they could be unofficially canonized, but during their lifetimes many suffered grievously.

But perhaps this treatment was not surprising: people persecute or ignore what they do not understand. And there was something particularly provoking about the Sufis. What, for instance, could a medieval theologian make of a man who called himself a mystic, was interested in man's evolution to a higher level, was associated with scientific work?

It is against this sort of historical background that it can be useful to view Sufi literature, which exists on many levels, from simple entertainment to truths that 'lie under the poet's tongue.' Codes and the cryptic had their practical, as well as their spiritual, uses.

Oriental studies even today are the Cinderella of the learned world. The reason for this is historical as well as the perennial difficulty that scholars who have cornered a market can refuse, or be unable, to recognize a real Sufi practitioner when one appears; even now our mental sets in the West exclude much factual information about the extent of the influence that Spain, the Arabs, the Moors – Islam – has had on our culture. This influence has been immense, if often not acknowledged at all. It is in this field that we can expect – it is already happening – startling results in academic research. But the block is there, and strong. Professor A. J. Arberry of Cambridge complains in a current book that someone trying to develop in this field 'should find himself on the defensive, that he should have to contend with cheap jibes, sometimes with active opposition.'[2]

The career of Idries Shah, who is the main current

2. *Oriental Essays* (London: G. Allen and Unwin 1960), p. 256.

exponent of Sufi literature and teaching, has in the past few years shown a resemblance to some of the classical Sufis. The same signs and symptoms of opposition have been seen; but there has also been support, and from the highest levels. Late in 1970, for instance, no sooner had the expected handful of irritated scholars opposed him, than a large body of experts set about writing a *Festschrift* (to be published by Cape). They included scholars from the West specializing in orientalism, and also many Orientals, covering between them the whole spectrum of oriental studies in which he works – Islamics, mysticism, Persian, Arabic, Turkish, Sufism, history. They include Arabs and Jews, and academics from both sides of the Iron Curtain, not to mention such people as diplomats, generals, a judge, and a cabinet minister who is also a Sufi authority in the Middle East.

The need for this type of active support can be encapsulated in a tale from the Mulla Nasrudin corpus:

> Nasrudin found a falcon sitting on his windowsill. He had never seen a bird of this kind before. 'You poor thing,' he said, 'how were you ever allowed to get into such a state?' He clipped the falcon's talons, cut its beak straight, and trimmed its feathers. 'Now you look more like a bird,' said Nasrudin.

There is also the problem that we are used to thinking of Eastern philosophies and their representatives through our Indian spectacles. 'Gurus' are teachers, are respected by the religious and scholarly establishments, are interviewed plentifully by journalists fascinated by their bizarre and obviously holy practices, are considered the more authentic the more they claim the things of this world are of no account. But Sufism does not resemble in any way what it considers to be a degeneration of a real tradition and says that you cannot approach Sufism until you are able to think that a person quite ordinary in appearance and in life can experience higher states of mind. Sufism believes itself to be the substance of that current which can develop man to a higher stage in his evolution. It is not contemptuous of the world. 'Be in the world, but not of it,' is the aim.

But the inability to believe in the combination of the mystic and the practical is not only of our time.

Roger Bacon, the Franciscan monk, lectured at Oxford from Sufi books in the thirteenth century: it was for his recommendation of Sufi practices that he got into trouble with the religious authorities. Lully of Majorca praised Sufi methodologies, was 'a devotee of Arabian mysticism' (Professor E. W. F. Tomlin). Today he finds a place in scientific literature as the inventor of a digital computer. Rumi, poet and mystic, stressed a theory of evolution eight hundred years before Darwin. Shabistari, a thirteenth-century Persian Sufi, writes of the mystic way while emphasizing the unbelievable power which could be released from the atom. El Ghazali wrote of the collective unconscious in relation to medical and psychological techniques. Hujwiri of India, at the time of the Norman Conquest of England, was writing (in a book about Sufi saints) that time and space are identical. Jafar Sadiq and Jabir (Geber), the fathers of Western chemistry, were Sufis. Baba Farid had commercial interests and Rumi had to defend him for it – as probably would have to be done today. For claiming that human enlightenment must be achieved by working with the material world, innumerable Sufis were isolated from potential wellwishers, because of the inculcated thought that they must be superficial if they lived ordinary lives and were concerned with the practical welfare of man. It is to be hoped that this ancient bias will not be strong enough to keep people's minds closed against what Sufism is offering now.

But less than ten years have achieved a remarkable soften-ing of prejudice. The first of Idries Shah's books, *The Sufis*, which becomes more extraordinary the more it is studied, because of its comprehensiveness, and because of what it is able to state openly about a subject which in its deeper reaches is by definition beyond verbalization, was accepted for review by the conventional literary establishment for the most part because of pressure from poets and other literary people; it was overlooked by academics in the field. Yet many people, on reading this book which nowhere stated that a 'school' was to start, that 'The Teaching' was being offered again, applied from all over the world to be students. This is a small example of the multi-sidedness of every Sufi activity and artifact. 'We are economical in our functioning,' say the Sufis. 'If you like, even parsimonious: everything we say, each thing we do, has many different functions and results.' A book which will continue as a standard reference book, which will be pasture for academics, is material for esoteric study, but made as dramatic an appearance as a man walking on to stage to blow a trumpet.

The new book, The *Magic Monastery*,[3] continues a theme. People who may ask: 'Right then, what is Sufism?' will find Sufism's 'taste' here. But it is also a textbook for students, if the word textbook is an appropriate word for activity which is not like anything that we have been taught to regard as study.

Sufism is a study which is not scholastic. Its materials are taken from almost every form of human experience. Its books and pens are in the environment and resemble nothing that the scholastic or the enthusiast even dream about. It is because recitations, effort and books are

3. Idries Shah, *The Magic Monastery* (London: Jonathan Cape, 1972).

included in this kind of study, and because Sufi teachers are called 'Teacher,' that the fact of a specialized communication has become confused with academic or imitative study. There is, therefore, 'Sufi study' and 'ordinary study' and the two are different. The position is as if 'mouse' and 'elephant' have both been given the same name. Up to a point (being quadrupeds, being grey, having tails) this inexactitude is of no moment. After that it is necessary to distinguish between the two. This distinguishing takes place in a Sufi Circle.[4]

This book, like some previous ones, consists of pieces of various lengths, each illustrating points, or themes, on various levels. Some are anecdotes, some parables, some are practically informative. But the book differs from its predecessors (except for *Reflections*, Octagon Press) in that Shah includes pieces specially written by himself to complete the book 'as a course in non-linear thinking.' In previous collections the emphasis has been on tales illustrating the instructional methods employed by sages during the last thousand years, taken from written and oral sources.

The Magic Monastery is particularly and intriguingly informative about methods used by a Teacher in active operation, who cannot always behave according to the contentions of ordinary social usage and politeness: his actions may be sharply at variance with both.

As, for instance, this: a famous nineteenth-century Sufi Teacher, Jan Fishan Khan, of Afghanistan, heard that a certain scholar was viciously attacking a neighbour. He invited both men to a feast, and, having asked the neighbour to react to nothing that might happen, when the feast was at its height he began to berate him as the scholar had done for

4. Idries Shah, *The Way of the Sufi* (London: Jonathan Cape, 1970).

iniquities and shortcomings of all sorts. The man kept silent, until the scholar cried, 'Please stop. I saw my own behaviour in you, and I cannot bear the sight.' Jan Fishan Khan said: 'In being here tonight we all took a chance. You that our friend here would not sit patiently but would attack you, I that you might be further inflamed by my vituperation instead of being shamed by it, and he that he might start to believe that I was really against him. Now we have solved the problem. The risk remains that the account of this interchange, passed from mouth to ear by those who do not know what we are doing, will represent our friend as weak, you as easily influenced, and me as easily angered.'

Such stuff is designed for – if you like – self-improvement; at least for self-observation. You don't have to be a formal student to make use of it. Nasrudin again: 'You have leather? You have thread and nails and dye and tools? Then why don't you make yourself a pair of shoes?'

A difficulty is that some people expect this material to be more sensational than it is; a Sufi would reply that our palates have been blunted; that we do not give gentle impacts a chance to operate; that people can put themselves at a remove from the Sufi operation by calling it 'banal.'

The necessity for a social or emotional ingredient in a teaching situation is denied by the Sufis, in sharp contradiction of other persuasions, whose advocates invariably, in theory or in reality, strive to include as many subjective and community ingredients as possible in 'teaching' contacts. An astonishing parallel to the Sufi insistence on the relatively greater power of subtle communication to affect man, is found in scientific work which shows that all living things, including man, are 'incredibly sensitive to waves of extraordinarily weak energy – when more robust influences are excluded.'[5]

Finally a piece from *The Magic Monastery*, which illustrates the first approach of many people to Sufism:

> There is a story about a man who went to a dictionary compiler and asked him why he was interested in money. The lexicographer was surprised and said: 'Wherever did you get that idea?'
>
> 'From your own writings,' said the visitor.
>
> 'But I have only written that one dictionary,' said the author.
>
> 'I know, and that is the book which I have read,' said the other man.
>
> 'But the book contains a hundred thousand words And out of those I don't suppose that more than twenty or thirty are about money.'
>
> 'What are you talking about all the other words for,' said the visitor, 'when *I* was asking you about the words for *money*?'

5. Idries Shah, *The Dermis Probe* (London: Jonathan Cape, 1971), Notes, quoting M. Gauquelin's *The Cosmic Clocks* (London: Peter Owen, 1967), which cites recent scientific work.

Vonnegut's Responsibility

Mother Night is the Vonnegut book that has not been reviewed anywhere, ever, because it was sold first into paperback for a handy sum: he needed the money for his large family. And paperbacks don't get reviewed, so it has been ordained. Authors always feel that readers should know and care more about this kind of literary imperative than they do; there is more to what makes reputations than is taught in classes on literature.

Mother Night is odd-man-out in another way, being a straight novel. You needn't realize this at once or, indeed, at all; for it is a tale as monstrous as we read in the newspapers. As early as page 4 we find an eighteen-year-old Jew who guards our criminal hero in a Jerusalem jail; he does not know the name of Joseph Goebbels, but insists that Tiglath-pileser the Third, an Assyrian who burned down Hazar (a small town in Israel) in 732, was a man remarkable enough to be remembered by educated humanity. This sort of homely detail, instantly recognizable as the stuff of our zaniness, transports us further than any space-time warp and does not really need the addition of Vonnegut's elegant fantasy to make Chimera Land.

The criminal here is an American, Howard W. Campbell Jr, an ordinary pleasant fellow, like us all. He was comfortably acclimatized, not being political by temperament, in Nazi Germany, but was recruited to be a spy for Us by an agent who recognized in him a fatal sense of the dramatic: he would never be able to resist seeing life as a battle between Good and Evil. During the war he invented and broadcast propaganda for the Nazis, while working reliably for Us. Fifteen years after the war, while living quietly with his memories in Greenwich Village he was caught, mostly because of his own feelings of guilt or puzzlement about who really had done what – a specifically Vonnegut identification with the ambiguities of complicity.

Irrational, of course; because, judged by what he had done he had been a very clever fellow and, indeed, a hero; and besides, he had survived, no mean achievement these days. His thoughts – well, they were another matter; and besides, he was no Eichmann or Calley to take orders and not know what it was he did: 'My case is different. I know when I tell a lie, am capable of imagining the cruel consequences of anybody's believing my lies, know cruelty is wrong. I could no more lie without noticing it than I could unknowingly pass a kidney stone.'

The force of Vonnegut's questioning is such that one has to sit down to think, to define degrees: Vonnegut simply cannot bear what we are, of course – like a lot of writers. The growl, the wince, the scream, that come off so many pages are due to this. But no other writer's sorrow, no other writer's refusal to play the child's game of Goodies and Baddies, is strong enough to make me remember, for instance, that before 1939 a great many people were shouting we should stop Hitler, that Nazism could be stopped if America and Britain wanted to. He makes me remember – he rubs our noses in the results of our missed chances – that when Nazism was not stopped, but flowered (to succumb to the associations of the word) into the expected and forecast war, how soon our judgements became warped by the horribleness of what was going on. The horribleness of the Nazis, of course: for almost at once

Good and Evil became polarized into Us and Them and quite forgotten was the knowledge that the war could have been prevented if our governments had wanted. What Vonnegut deals with, always, is responsibility: Whose fault was it all – the gas chambers, the camps, the degradations, and the debasements of all our standards? Whose? Well, *ours* as much as *theirs*.

This is so, that is, if you can believe in responsibility at all – it is here that Vonnegut is moral in an old-fashioned way. He does take the full weight of responsibility, while more and more people are shrugging off the *we should have* and *we ought to have* and *we can if we want* and coming to see history as a puppet show and our – humanity's – slide into chaos as beyond our prevention, our will, our choice. The strength of Kurt Vonnegut Jr, this deliberate and self-conscious heir, derives from his refusal to succumb to this new and general feeling of helplessness.

There is another way he is an original: for most of his career he has been in the category 'space fiction' or 'science fiction,' where, for the most part, the chilliness of space derives from the writers' insistence that we do without the comforts of our own patterns of ethic, where we can see whole galaxies crumble with less emotion than we feel pouring boiling water into an ants' nest. Usually, in the centre of Jex 132 (male) or Janni X56 (female) there is an emptiness which some claim is the proper imaginative response to the possibilities of all space, but which in Vonnegut's people is filled with the emotions you and I would feel if we knew a molecule was loose that will freeze our world solid in a breath.

Precisely because in all his work he has made nonsense of the little categories, the unnatural divisions into 'real' literature and the rest, because he is comic and sad at once, because his painful seriousness is never solemn, Vonnegut is unique among us; and these same qualities account for the way a few academics still try to patronize him: they cling to the categories. Of course they do: they invented them. But so it has ever been.

Ordinary people, with whole imaginations, reading the newspapers, the comic strips, and Jane Austen or watching the world reel by on television, keep an eye out for Ice 9 while hoping that we are indeed recognizing the members of our *karasses* when they come near, try to make sure that we don't pay more than what is due to the false *karasses*, and dare to believe that while there is life, there is still life – such readers know that Vonnegut is one of the writers who map our landscapes for us, who give names to the places we know best.

Ant's Eye View: A Review of
The Soul of the White Ant
by Eugène Marais

This book has had a struggling stubborn life, like its author.
He was Eugène Neilen Marais, born in 1871 into a farming
community near Pretoria 'as completely cut off from the
civilised world as the loneliest island in the Pacific.' He was
Dutch and Huguenot – an Afrikaner. He was critical of an
English-influenced education and of the English, whom he
was then able to admire. He was first a journalist, already
consciously developing the new language, Afrikaans, and
became editor of *Land en Volk*. His career as Parliamentary
Reporter ended when he was excluded from the Press Gallery
by resolution of a touchy *Volksraad*. He was indicted for
high treason for attacking Paul Kruger, but the Pretoria
Supreme Court acquitted him. He married at twenty-two.
His wife died a year later, leaving a son. He was introduced
to morphine, probably through his fascination with medicine. But friends advised him to study law, which he went to
England to do.

He graduated as the Boer War began – the war that had
been inevitable ever since the discovery of the wealth of the
Transvaal. Marais was suddenly an enemy alien in England
but escaped to Central Africa, from where he smuggled arms
and medicaments to the Boers. The brutality of the British
troops sickened him; for a long time he would not write in
English. Becoming solitary, he went to the Waterberg
mountains and began his study of animals in their environ-

ment. He lived with wild chacma baboons for three years. Long before Lorenz, he pioneered this science, working without libraries, without training, not knowing what others in the field were doing. But his isolation was the saving of an original genius whose intellectual loneliness (painful to feel in his writing even now) might have allowed him to take advice from much littler men. This period resulted in *My Friends the Baboons*, a collection of newspaper pieces for whose lack of science he later apologized though they are marvellously alive, and, much later, the scientific work, *The Soul of the Ape*. Leaving his mountains he became poet, journalist, advocate, justice of the peace, scientist. He was mostly solitary, the prey of malaria and morphine.

He studied animals, and was preoccupied with the nature of the human soul, or psyche, or mind. There is currently an academic reaction away from admiration of Lorenz and the like-minded. It would be nice to think this was more than old hostility of the laboratory for the field, or the older dislike of admitting our closeness to animals. Which likeness flatters us rather than not, some people think. It is one thing to say: 'Man is not all animal,' with a jealousy for his humanity, but it can be conceit, and lead to the savagery with which we treat animals, or so I believe. It is another to say: 'Whatever of man that is not shared with animals is intermingled with the animal like spice in a cake mix, and it doesn't do to get above ourselves.' Marais's baboon studies led him to the view, then new among European philosophers, since common, that man is in unrest (and due for extinction) because his older brain fights with his civilized morality. His comparison of a termitary with a human being was a worm's – or ant's – eye view, most easily compared to the sf stories where shrunken people go voyaging along veins and arteries, through valves, and among hearts, livers, and lights like great animals or like countries, in a continent or an orchestra of

208

individually working units all held together by an invisible force 'like electricity.'

The articles that he meant to make into a book were printed in a widely circulating magazine, and Maurice Maeterlinck, the world-famous writer and Nobel prize-winner, stole them and published them under the title *Life of the White Ant*, in 1926. Protests from publishers, even diplomatic intervention, did not break Maeterlinck's silence, or bring help from literary figures who might have been expected to feel concern. Perhaps they thought South Africa was too far away to matter. The blow must have contributed to Marais's black miseries, his addiction, and his suicide in 1936.

The Soul of the White Ant was published here in English in 1937, largely through the efforts of Dr Winifred de Kok, his translator. Her foreword began the business of putting things right. Robert Ardrey and others have helped here and in America. This edition is almost a reproduction of that one. It is a pity there is not a fuller introduction, that the cover looks like one of Marais's depressions, that there is no picture of that unforgettable face. A pity, in short, that more trouble wasn't taken over a book that has been a powerful influence in our time. It is unique, rough, tough, shaped like a root by the necessities of its growth. Marais's analogy of the termitary with the human body, an organism of which the queen ant is the soul, or breath, invisibly controlling workers, soldiers, the fungus gardens, the galleries, hard outer shell (skin, streams of blood, organs), is only a jumping-off place for inspired speculation. A termitary *is* an animal. Immobile, of course . . . Then he cracks our thought habits by an invitation to imagine it in movement, but in a time scale different from ours, as if we were able to see the movements of ice in the contractions and expansions of an ice age. He offers a vision of Nature as a whole, whose parts obey different time laws, move in affinities and linkages we could learn to see, parts making wholes on their own level, but seen by our divisive brains as a multitude of individualities, a flock of birds, a species of plant or beast—man. We are just at the start of an understanding of the heavens as a web of interlocking clocks, all differently set: an understanding that is not intellectual but woven into experience. Marais brings this thought down into the plain, the hedgerow, a garden.

In such insights Marais catapults out of his time and ahead of ours. But it is a smaller, commoner human plaint that is the ground of his work: 'When we make our deepest feelings the arbiter we are dismayed. For we seek in vain in nature for love, sympathy, pity, justice, altruism, protection of the innocent and weak. Pain is the condition of existence. Escape from pain is the purpose of all striving.' Olive Schreiner could have written that. She did, in different words.

Marais was solitary, but one of a scattered band of South Africans bred out of the veld, self-hewn, in advance of their time – and paying heavily for it. Schreiner was one, always fighting, always ill. Bosman another, the journalist and short-story writer who wrote the saddest of all prison books, *Cold Stone Jug*. His account of how hundreds of prisoners howled like dogs or hyenas through their bars at the full moon – everyone, warders too, pretending afterwards that it had never happened, has the same ring to it as Marais's description of the baboons screaming out their helplessness through the night after leopards had carried off one of their troop.

A Deep Darkness: A Review of
Out of Africa
by Karen Blixen

Karen Blixen was a Dane and a baroness. She identified with sea adventurers. Also with the nobility, noble behaviour. By heredity, experience, temperament, she was an enemy of the commonplace, and it is not surprising she became a Kenyan coffee farmer – even now a hard thing for a young woman to be alone, and with little money. That was 1913 and she was twenty-eight. The farm was too high for good coffee, there were years of drought and locusts, finally the slump. She was bankrupt and went back to Denmark in 1931. *Out of Africa* is twenty years of her life; but it is only when you work things out that you find she must have been at such an age when she did this or thus – fifty, when she left Kenya – that you understand the book's special quality, of a tale much concentrated, like a myth.

Partly this is because of her feeling for the past, her own life being seen as a small putting-forth from the root of her ancestry – which is how the Africans she lived among saw theirs – and partly because there is nothing in it of the grind of one day after another. It is all distillation; and happiness, pain, this or that bit of luck or misfortune, are parts of a pattern or plot. By the best of script writers, of course, if not Cervantes, then Conrad, whose view of people as items in a high drama she shares. The players on her stage are white, black, brown. On her farm lived the Kikuyu. The Masai were across the river. Her major-domo and friend was Farah, a

Somali. She enjoyed the company of the Indian merchants from Nairobi and Mombasa. She quotes: 'Noble found I ever the Native and insipid the Immigrant,' complaining that while the natives, because of their long contact with raiding and trading Arabs and Indians, are cosmopolitan, the whites are provincial. Except, of course, for her small band of special friends.

Casually she allows to emerge the picture of a young woman living in a house with doors opening onto a terrace, beyond which are lawns with great trees under which she sits to palaver with chiefs and commoners. Beyond these the river, plains, the Ngong hills. She was alone in Eden save for the deerhounds, and the bushbuck Lulu, for whom they would give up their places by the fire. Proud that her table was the best in the Colony, she gave dinner parties, danced, rode, shot. She hints it was a callous or careless young woman who was ground into maturity, but does not make much of either state, since growth is to be expected of people. Her guests were mostly men. Needing the company of women, she sat at sundown in the house of Farah, whose womenfolk were her especial friends. For her real life was not the social one, but with 'her people' – particularly Farah; the boy Kamante, whom she saved from crippledom and whom she taught to be a great chef; the farm's women, and Chief Kinanjui the Kikuyu. All these understood so well where she belonged in heart that when she emerged from a time of personal crisis, or from writing, they spoke thus: 'When you were away'; or 'That tree fell down, my child died, while you were with the white people.'

This being so feudal fitted her well for that epoch of younger sons living on mortgages off vast farms, with innocently open-hearted Africans. But that ended with indiscriminate white immigration. Newcomers called "The Mayflower People' arrogant. She says they were blind.

Nine thousand feet up we felt safe and we laughed at the ambition of the new arrivals, the Missions, the business people and the Government itself, to make the Continent of Africa respectable.

She mentions a husband, once. What she wants to say about loving friendship is in accounts of Berkeley Cole and Denys Finch-Hatton who made her house their own. Berkeley had his own farm, but preferred hers; whereas Denys never had a home, but, like Virginia Woolf's Orlando's lover, was always on safari. These two men kept her in wine, ordered her books and records from Europe, inspired Kamante with comparison from the great houses and restaurants of Europe. They were self-conscious, self-parodying dandies. Berkeley Cole drank a bottle of champagne under her trees each morning at eleven, and complained, being given coarse and vulgar glass, since she did not want her good glass broken, 'But, my dear . . . it has been so sad.' Thereafter they always used the best glass. He died, and people dated an epoch from it: 'While Berkeley Cole was alive.' He should have been a Cavalier; and Denys Finch-Hatton, really an Elizabethan, taught her Latin and Greek; taught himself to fly so that she might see Africa from the air, and, loving music, said he could have liked Beethoven if he were not so vulgar. One New Year they sat at a table made of a millstone brought from India by merchants, and saw the moon, Venus, Jupiter radiantly together. Once she was at tea when he descended from the sky in his Moth, saying she must come to see buffalo feeding in the hills. She protested her guests, but he promised to have her back in fifteen minutes, and she was, having seen buffalo, sky, and hills.

All this time she got poorer, and when he knew she must leave, Denys refused to take her on a trip to the coast – and he had never refused before – and he crashed and was buried

in the Ngong hills. On the plateau where his grave is, lions
came to sit and gaze over plains where soon would creep the
suburbs of Nairobi. As Denys said, refusing a house in such a
suburb, when people felt he ought not to be always in a tent
or in the air, 'This continent of Africa has a very fine sense of
sarcasm.' To the end she fought for her farm, and fought,
too, for 'her people' against the ravages of the new creed:
Teach the Native to want; and against white officialdom. For
while the idea that a man has rights was not one she could
hold, she could not stand that he should be hurt or insulted.

The plot of this drama isn't important. If it had been: she
came to Africa, farmed successfully, pleased the respectable –
it would have been the same. For the book is not 'about'
anything but Africa:

> The sweet noble black of Africa, deep darkness absorbed
> through age, like old soot, that makes you feel that for
> elegance, vigour and vivacity, no colours rival black.

About what lies behind the words heard always when black
men are first shocked by white, the epitaph, 'White men are
very clever, but they have no hearts.' About the landscape:
rivers, hills, plains, creatures. When she was back in
Denmark old servants wrote to her: 'Honourable Lioness,' as
they had called Denys Finch-Hatton a lion, and knew that
she thought of them and would soon be back with them. She
did not have the money, though she dreamed of going back
to start a school, or a hospital.

Instead she wrote a sequel, *Shadows on the Grass*, out of
love and homesickness, recalling Farah in particular, who,
when at the end she was so poor she had no furniture in her
house, put on all the magnificence of his best clothes to open
doors onto empty rooms and to walk behind her as she went
begging from office to office for 'her' Kikuyu – the land had

been bought to build villas on. No, she never saw that her 6,000 acres was not hers, and that it was not enough to call the Kikuyu squatters (similarly, masters, servants, lions, kings, chameleons) even if she did count herself a squatter with them.

In the postscript book are two photographs, one of a young beauty so sure of herself she is in sloppy khaki trousers and a man's hat, the only elegance being a deerhound half her height. The other is of a crone which, when I first saw it, made me want to shout to her: How can you! – the way women do when they feel another is letting the side down. But now the decades have begun to tick past I understand the relish with which I am sure she juxtaposed the two. She and the jocose old Kikuyu women who had lived through to the other side of happiness and pain had the closest of silent understandings. She approved, before the Government forbade it, the Kikuyu way of putting out their dead to be cleaned to the bone by vultures and hyenas, death being one with life and neither more than a process. A noble one – of course, for everything is, and nothing without meaning; which is why she is on so many people's special shelf, to be taken down more and more often as an antidote to our eleventh hour of squalid destructiveness.

The chief feature of the landscape, and of your life in it, was the air. Looking back on a sojourn in the African highlands, you are struck by your feeling of having lived for a time up in the air. The sky was rarely more than pale blue or violet, with a profusion of white, weightless, ever-changing clouds towering up and sailing on it, but it has a blue vigour in it, and at a short distance it painted the ranges of the hills and the woods a fresh deep blue. In the middle of the day the air was alive over the land like a flame burning: it scintillated, waved, and shone like running water, mirrored and doubled all objects, and created great Fata Morgana. Up in this high air you breathed easily, drawing in a vital assurance and lightness of heart. In the highlands you woke up in a morning and thought: Here am I, where I ought to be.

On Africa

Being Prohibited

A large number of my friends are locked out of countries and unable to return; locked into countries and unable to get out; have been deported, prohibited, and banned. Among this select company I can now hold up my head. I am troubled, however, by secret doubts.

Before planning my trip to South Africa, it crossed my mind to wonder whether I should be allowed in; humility checked me. What have I, in fact, done to the Union government? In 1947 when I was on holiday, I worked for the *Guardian* in Cape Town for two months, as a typist. The *Guardian*, like the *Daily Worker* now, was in permanent financial crisis; and that brave band of people, the finance committee, sat in almost continuous session, wondering how to pay for the next issue and muttering enviously about Moscow gold. I wrote a lot of letters for this committee.

In 1949, on my way through to England, I undeniably consorted with people since named as communists. Some were, some were not.

Of course, since I joined the Communist Party in England I have made no secret of the fact; but the idea that MI5 would send warnings to South Africa of my approach seems to border on megalomania. This state of mind was ably described by a friend of mine who not only believed that the sword was mightier than the pen, but acted on it. An admirable person, he said that his chief handicap as an

219

agitator was that at moments of crisis he could never really believe he was about to be arrested, because he was obviously right in his views and surely everyone must agree with him when it came to the point. My friend also used to say that the main fault of the left was that we continually ascribe our own intelligence and high-mindedness to our opponents. Apropos, I remember that once, by a series of mischances, I spent an evening with the backroom boys of the Nationalist Party. It was a salutary experience. I still find it hard to believe that such cynical oafs can keep a whole sub-continent in thrall.

Some weeks before leaving England this time, I was visited by two people, deported from South Africa, who told me I was mad to think I would be allowed in and that I was politically very naïve. Almost immediately afterwards, came another visitor, a political *émigré* of a superior kind who has for some years now been conducting a really epic fight with the Nationalists.

He said: 'What's this I hear? What makes you think *you* are so dangerous that you won't be allowed in? You ought to be ashamed of yourself. You are on the official list of South African authors at South Africa House.' It will be seen why I was in a confused state of mind when I left England.

I had worked out a really cunning plot to enter the Union: it depended on an intimate knowledge of the habits of their immigration officials. This plot was received with amusement by my friends in Salisbury, who suggested I was suffering from a persecution complex. Not for one moment do I blame them for their attitude: the atmosphere of Southern Rhodesia, in contrast with the troubled territories north and south, is one of good humour. Everybody one meets says how efficient the CID is and that nothing one does ever escapes them; but it is rather as one speaks of a benevolent uncle. And I have it on the highest possible authority that the leaders of the Africans in that country are both "pleasant and

220

sound.' No, I have no doubt that if I lived again in Salisbury, within six months I should be talking about troublemakers and agitators with the best.

Lulled, therefore, into a state of innocence, I spent four days seeing old friends and reviving the sundowner habit before actually flying south. In the aircraft there was plenty of time for reminiscence: that first time, for instance, that I entered the Union, in 1937 . . .

The border is Mafeking, a little dorp with nothing interesting about it but its name. The train waits (or used to wait) interminably on the empty tracks, while immigration and customs officials made their leisurely way through the coaches, and pale gritty dust settled over everything. Looking out, one saw the long stretch of windows, with the two, three, or four white faces at each; then at the extreme end, the single coach for 'natives' packed tight with black humans; and, in between, two or three Indians or Coloured people on sufferance in the European coaches. Outside, on the scintillating dust by the tracks, a crowd of ragged black children begged for *bonsellas*. One threw down sandwich crusts or bits of spoiled fruit and watched them dive and fight to retrieve them from the dirt.

I was sixteen. I was not, as one says, politically conscious; nor did I know the score. I knew no more, in fact, than on which side my bread was buttered. But I already felt uneasy about being a member of the Herrenvolk. When the immigration official reached me, I had written on the form: *Nationality*, British, *Race*, European; and it was the first time in my life I had had to claim myself as a member of one race and disown the others. I remember distinctly that I had to suppress an impulse opposite *Race*: Human. Of course I *was* very young.

The immigration man had the sarcastic surliness which characterizes the Afrikaans official, and he looked

suspiciously at my form for a long time before saying that I
was in the wrong part of the train. I did not understand him.
(I forgot to mention that where the form asked, Where were
you born?, I had written, Persia.)

'Asiatics,' said he, 'have to go to the back of the train; and
anyway you are prohibited from entry unless you have
documents proving you conform to the immigration quota
for Asians.'

'But,' I said, 'I am not an Asiatic.'

The compartment had five other females in it; skirts were
visibly being drawn aside. To prove my bona fides I should,
of course, have exclaimed with outraged indignation at any
such idea.

'You were born in Persia?'

'Yes.'

'Then you are an Asiatic. You know the penalties for filling
in the form wrongly?'

This particular little imbroglio involved my being taken off
the train, escorted to an office, and kept under watch while
they telephoned Pretoria for a ruling.

When next I entered the Union it was 1939. Sophistication
had set in in the interval, and it took me no more than five
minutes to persuade the official that one could be born in a
country without being its citizen. The next two times there
was no trouble at all, although my political views had in the
meantime become nothing less than inflammatory: in a word,
I had learned to disapprove of the colour bar.

This time, two weeks ago, what happened was as follows:
one gets off the plane and sits for about fifteen minutes in a
waiting room while they check the plane list with a list, or
lists, of their own. They called my name first, and took me to
an office which had two tables in it. At one sat a young man
being pleasant to the genuine South African citizens. At the
one where they made me sit was a man I could have sworn I

had seen before. He proceeded to go through my form item by item, as follows: 'You *say*, Mrs Lessing, that, etc . . .' From time to time he let out a disbelieving laugh and exchanged ironical looks with a fellow official who was standing by. Sure enough, when he reached that point on my form when he had to say: 'You *claim* that you are British; you *say* you were born in Persia,' I merely said 'Yes,' and sat still while he gave me a long, exasperated stare. Then he let out an angry exclamation in Afrikaans and went next door to telephone Pretoria. Ten minutes later I was informed I must leave at once. A plane was waiting and I must enter it immediately.

I did so with dignity. Since then I have been unable to make up my mind whether I should have made a scene or not. I never have believed in the efficacy of dignity.

On the plane I wanted to sit near the window but was made to sit by myself and away from the window. I regretted infinitely that I had no accomplices hidden in the long grass by the airstrip, but, alas, I had not thought of it beforehand.

It was some time before it came home to me what an honour had been paid me. But now I am uneasy about the whole thing: suppose that I owe these attentions, not to my political views, but to the accident of my birth place?

Mr Donges was asked about the incident, but all he said was, 'No comment.'[1]

---

1. T. E. Donges (1898-1968), South African Minister of the Interior (1948-58) and Finance Minister (1958-66). Elected President of South Africa in 1968, he died before being inaugurated.

The Fruits of Humbug

The Federation mentioned here is the Central African Federation, an association which existed between 1954 and the early 1960s, of Nyasaland, now Malawi; Northern Rhodesia, now Zambia; and Southern Rhodesia, now Rhodesia. This Federation was from the first opposed by the Africans of all three territories, but their wishes were ignored by the white settlers and by the Conservative and Labour Parties of Great Britain. The Federation ended in bitterness and violence, as it was bound to do. Going Home *describes a trip to Rhodesia and Northern Rhodesia in 1956 at a time when African resistance to the Federation was at its height.*

Today an accident occurred which, for lovers of the bizarre, has a high quality of improbability that makes it a connoisseur's item. This afternoon's *Star* (March 3) has the headline: 'Banned MP Deported. Carried Struggling Aboard Plane.' If one read no further, then almost certainly the supposition would be that some mind-improving member of Parliament on a jaunt to China or the Soviet Union had strayed from the delegation and been caught furtively photographing a ball-bearings plant; or some subject equally fraught with malicious possibilities, such as a beggar, or similar backward element; or the expression on Boris Pasternak's face as he catches sight of yet another helpful journalist. I can imagine myself hurrying through the crowds along Oxford Street thinking: "What! One of *our* members of Parliament *struggling*! Impossible. What will the Russians think of such lack of poise?' When being deported, it is assumed one should go with dignity, as to the guillotine.

But the story continues: "Mr John Stonehouse, the British Labour MP, was deported from Northern Rhodesia today. He was carried struggling by immigration officials aboard a Government plane.' Etc.

The point is that Northern Rhodesia, like Nyasaland, is still in theory under the control of the British Parliament. The Federal authorities have deported from their territory a person who is a member of the body that is supposed to govern it.

And he struggled. Good. I now very much regret that when I was deported from South Africa I did not struggle. Admittedly, escorted as I was by a posse of plainclothes men, concerned that I should not – perhaps? – escape, I would not have been allowed to struggle long. But it would have been a gesture.

I had no opportunity to struggle when declared a prohibited immigrant in the Federation for the good reason that I was not informed of this event at the time. I read with interest in some newspaper this week that Welensky says that when declared a prohibited immigrant, one has twenty-four hours in which to appeal. But how can one appeal when not informed of one's status? I shouldn't imagine that the Federal authorities gave much thought to this legal anomaly. They are not troubled by details. More, I'm prepared to bet that at the moment when the Governor-in-Council signed the order there were tears of outraged and reproachful emotion in his eyes. How can she – he, or they, were thinking – how can she behave in such a way as to force us into this position? It makes such a bad impression on the outside world, which never understands us.

It appears, actually, that I was prohibited some years ago, they forgot to inform me, and, when I went back two years ago, they let me in by accident. So I'm told by reliable though indirect information. The point is, they are very unhappy having to do these things. I remember when I went down to the Immigration Officer in London, in a final attempt to get some positive information about my status, it was only after several minutes of close questioning on my part that I could get the clear statement that I was, in fact, declared a prohibited immigrant. 'You've forced my hand,' he exclaimed tragically. I could hear him thinking: Oh drat it, why does she have to put us in this distressing position?

Similarly, knowing my compatriots (white) as I do, I'm pretty sure that at this moment, five o'clock, March 3, they are discussing Mr Stonehouse all over the Federation with hatred and disgust, certainly, but also with an element of baffled reproach. 'After all, he's a white man, isn't he? Why does he want to embarrass us?' They won't be actually saying this, because in all states where the virtuous left hand is careful not to notice what the unscrupulous right hand does, people don't express their deepest emotions. Right now, in the Federation, they will be feeling misunderstood and ill-treated.

That they are misunderstood in this country (though not in the way they think) is certainly true. I'm always being asked to explain some incident or other to puzzled people who have no difficulty at all in understanding South Africa. The Union of South Africa is straightforward. For the last ten years its Government has been engaged in passing laws and creating a state where a dark-skinned person is not much better than a slave, and telling the world, with an admirable lack of hypocrisy, exactly what they are doing.

Not so the Federation, which confuses everyone, including itself, by murmuring incantatory words like 'partnership,' and making shocked noises about the goings-on in the Union.

For instance, in the Union a black person may not marry a white person. In the Federation he may. Only one couple actually tried it. An African married a white woman, but although this was legal there was no place in the Federation they might legally set up house together. They took refuge at St Faith's Mission, to the accompaniment of protest meetings by the local whites. Guy Clutton-Brock, who runs St Faith's, was arrested last week. Such is the fate of those who run counter to the spirit of partnership, whose aim is in fact to maintain white supremacy – whose essence is humbug. The British, as we all admit, are masters of humbug, and this our child, the Central African Federation, is a very highly developed expression of it. Therefore people in this country ought not really to be so confused by the place.

The anomalies, the highhandedness, the high hot emotions of Central Africa are all the result of the humbug inherent in the mere existence of Federation.

Admittedly a good deal existed before. An incident occurred when I was a child which I think should make it clear what I mean.

This happened on a maize farm. One of the farm labourers wanted to leave before the expiration of a month's contract. He was dissatisfied with the conditions of the work. These conditions were: payment, 12*s* 6*d* a month; a ration of maize-meal and beans; a mud hut to live in; heavy physical labour from six in the morning until six at night with an hour's break.

It happened that this man was an hour late for work one morning after a beer drink. The farmer fined him 2*s* – that is, a sixth of a month's wages. So he asked to leave. The farmer said no; he was short of labour. So the labourer ran away, but unluckily was seen in the compound of a neighbouring farmer, who sent him back.

Now it is not allowed that white people should beat their employees. They do, of course, but the correct procedure is, if an employee offends, to take him to the nearest police station where he will be given the option of being beaten by the African constable or fined, probably 10s. (Nearly a month's wage.) The offender very often chooses to be beaten. It is much cheaper. (Things of course are better than they used to be – farm labourers can earn £3 or £4 a month, and they often get meat with their maizemeal.)

And so now occurred a remarkable conversation to which I remember listening – I was about twelve at the time – with a sense of improbability that has never left me since. There sat the farmer on his chair on the verandah and before him stood the culprit, guarded by the boss-boy. 'Elias, this won't do, you know.'

'Baas?'

'I'm very busy, it's the wet season and I can't afford to take the afternoon off to drive into the police station.'

'Baas.'

'If I take you to the police now, your name will be in the records. You do realize that?'

'Baas.'

'We'll make a bargain. You let me order the boss-boy to give you a good hiding and we'll call it quits. Hey?'

'No baas. Take me to the police station.'

'Damn it, man, every time I leave the farm for even half an hour, it's hundreds of pounds down the drain, the moment my back is turned you black swine stop working.'

'Baas.'

'Elias, the boss-boy's right here. It'll be over in five minutes. What do you say ?'

'Baas, if you beat me I tell the police and they'll fine you.'

'*What?*' Aside, to his wife: 'There, did you hear that? It's the influence of those kaffir-lovers in Westminster. If they'd only get it into their heads that the only language the blacks understood is the whip. What nonsense, not being allowed to hit our own blacks.'

"I want to leave, baas.'

"Well, you're not leaving. You signed a contract. You've got to give a month's notice.'

'Then take me to the police.'

The farmer looked at him with sheer, blank, irritable incredulity. 'God damn it, man, Elias – do you realize you are forcing me to lose my temper?'

'Baas.'

The farmer, crying aloud to the hostile heavens: 'My God, and they expect us to make a profit. My God, these black swine don't understand the first thing about modern conditions, they don't even accept a contract, and those fools in England talk about giving them equality. My God, when will they understand our problems?'

Right now, all over the Federation, bitter white settlers will be exclaiming that we (the British) don't understand their problems. They will not, however, since humbug has taken so deep a root, be mentioning profits at all.

That is why I am so glad that Mr Stonehouse struggled. The story might have read: British MP deported from Federation. And we are so used to deportations, prohibitions, and the rest that it makes no impact. *Struggle* is a good, lively word that brings a situation to life. During the last few days, while the crisis mounted, I've been reading the newspapers and marvelling how easy it is for words to obscure a situation.

For instance: 'Police swoop at night and arrest several dozen Congress leaders.' People in this country, I should imagine, would form a mental image of a dozen nice-mannered navy-blue policemen, knocking on the door: Sir, Madam, perhaps you would accompany me to the police station. I must warn you that anything you say, etc.

Not so in Central Africa. When the Congress leaders were arrested a week ago in Southern Rhodesia – it will be recalled that this was done before the Congress had actually taken any action – lorry loads of armed men arrived without warning in the middle of the night and broke forcibly into houses in the African townships. When I say houses, I mean brick-enclosed spaces the size of a well-treated dog's kennel. When I say township, I mean the segregated ghettos in which Africans have to live, since it is against the law for them to live on white land. They were shouted at, abused, beaten up, and dragged off to jail. Charge? But this was a preventive measure.

This method of dealing with situations is commonplace in these parts. When the Northern Rhodesian Government broke the strike on the Copper Belt in 1956, the authorities swooped at midnight and took their victims off with them to jails in the bush by lorry. They arrested, at the same time, quite a few Congressmen, who in fact had had nothing to do with the strike, just for good measure, and because it was a good opportunity to get rid of than. At the time it was hard to find out exactly how many were taken – figures fluctuated wildly from fifty to a hundred for a few days; the Federal authorities can never understand why one should make a fuss about a dozen blacks, one way or the other. When *habeas corpus* was invoked and a court decided the whole affair had been illegal, the Legislative Council made it retroactively legal by passing a law the same afternoon.

The state of the law in the Federation is in fact a most ambiguous and convenient thing for the authorities. I notice that Welensky said that the Southern Rhodesian Congress leaders he arrested had criminal records. This does not mean what you might suppose. The Congress leaders in Northern Rhodesia have criminal records too. Harry Nkumbula and

Kenneth Kaunda have both done time for being in possession of prohibited literature – the *W.F.T.U. Journal*, as I recall – but anything is possible, perhaps it was the *New Statesman*. In fact, for an African not to have some kind of police record shows he must be a remarkably ingenious person. As in the Union of South Africa, there are so many passes and permits one must carry, so many regulations to infringe, the curfew, areas a black man may not be in, that an African can be arrested at any time, because he is bound to have broken some law or other by the very nature of his existence.

Another phrase that has been in use the last week is *hard core*. Actually this is more a colonial phrase than a British one. At least, if it were said here that the *hard core* of a strike were, or was, taken into custody, one could assume that some kind of court procedure had been used. *Hard core*, used of places like Kenya, Cyprus, or any British overseas possession, means any person about at the time who has been giving trouble.

There was labour trouble at the Wankie collieries in '55 or '56. It happened that I saw the verbatim transcript of the hearing – which had been held without the benefit of outside witnesses, impartial or otherwise. A curious document. There had been, of course, an agent provocateur, spies, etc.; also beatings-up and intimidation and finally the *hard core* had simply been taken off and dumped over the border under threat of imprisonment if they returned. When they arrested the hard core at Kariba last week, this meant that any labourer who showed any signs at all of disapproving of his conditions was rounded up and bundled out of sight.

Highhanded, as I've said. There is a fine contempt for concepts like law, liberty, etc., that people in this country, spoiled as they are by their traditions, must find it hard to understand. Therefore, it should be the duty of the newspapers to explain it to them.

232

Two years ago, when I returned from the Federation after a six weeks' visit, I found it impossible to convince any newspapers but *Tribune* and the *New Statesman* that the Federation was heading for bad trouble. Soothing words like *partnership* were murmured, with the suggestion that one was being perhaps unfair. After all, the Federation was a fine new exercise in human relations.

But what is the Federation? Southern Rhodesia, a self-governing colony, is extremely similar in legal structure, atmosphere and colour-bar attitudes to the Union of South Africa, which it adjoins. But the Afrikaans Nationalists now have the Union in their grip, and British Southern Rhodesia wanted to link itself northwards to prevent itself being absorbed by the Union. North is Nyasaland and Northern Rhodesia. Both countries are British protectorates under the Colonial Office. In both the Africans saw themselves as temporary wards, destined to progress slowly towards self-government. The colour-bar restrictions were much less stringent and there was more freedom. But above all – and this is the basic fact that I have not seen printed anywhere during the last two weeks of crisis – in Northern Rhodesia and Nyasaland the land rights of the Africans have been more or less respected. They have lost about 6 per cent of their land to the whites. In Southern Rhodesia the whites have taken two-thirds of the land. That is, in two-thirds of their own country the Africans may not live, save in segregated townships, move without permission of the police, or own land. This fundamental fact is what the Africans saw when threatened with Federation. They knew that handed over to Southern Rhodesia and Welensky, they would slowly lose their land to the whites, slowly lose what liberties they still possessed.

The masses of the Africans in both territories resisted Federation. To soothe them and delude the outside world, the word *partnership* was invented. The Africans were not deluded. Many people here who should have known better were.

The growth of the National Congresses in all three territories is a direct result of the fact that Federation was forced on the Africans against their will.

I continue this article on March 4. Yesterday, twenty-six Africans were shot by white troops. The leadership of the Nyasaland Congress has been arrested and deported.

The word Mau-mau is already being used to justify the white settlers.

I see that, after carefully reading the newspapers, they have not seen fit to mention what surely is a key fact, that the annual average income for Africans in Nyasaland is £3 10s a year.

Instead, the familiar jargon of 'agitators,' 'power-hungry black leaders,' 'thugs,' etc., is being used.

By the time this article is printed one of two things will have happened in the Federation. The Nationalist movements in all three territories will have been so completely and ruthlessly suppressed that the Africans will be left silenced and sullen. A few stooges will be paraded by the Federal Government to prove that all is well. The jails and detention camps will be full. They will remain full. (Some of the trade unionists arrested on the Copper Belt in '56 are still detained without proper trial.) It will be a country of simmering resentments, race hatred, always on the verge of explosion.

Alternatively, violence in ugly shapes will erupt sporadically. When the leadership of an African movement is arrested and the masses are left without guidance, they turn to bitter, desperate, and bloody men. This is one of the hard political facts of our time. We have the object lesson of

Kenya. It is my belief that the Federal authorities have arrested the leaders of the Congresses hoping that violent outbreaks will occur, so that they can discredit the whole nationalist movement by using words like Mau-mau.

But whatever happens it is our responsibility. We, the British electorate, allowed our Government to hand over to Sir Roy Welensky, who privately claims virtues for the South African system, the Africans of Nyasaland and Northern Rhodesia, against their will, and in betrayal of promises made to them by us.

We are responsible for one of the ugliest social systems in the world, where seven million Africans live in conditions of extreme poverty, ridden by disease, malnutrition, illiteracy, kept in segregated townships and reserves, deprived of even the pretence of liberty. They are ruled by 300,000 whites, whose standards of living are higher than those of all but a tiny minority of the British people, and who are prepared to do anything to maintain their privileges.

These are the facts. During the next few months, when it is likely that we will be thinking of Central Africa as 'another Kenya,' or perhaps a distant trouble spot, we should remember that it is our responsibility, the fruit of years of humbug and double-talk.

NOTE FROM THE AUTHOR

I have changed my mind about politics since I wrote these essays. More recent pieces are available in a new collection of interviews entitled *Doris Lessing: Conversations*.

Paul Schlueter, the editor of this collection, taught university-level English for many years in the United States as well as in Germany; he now devotes his time to various writing and editorial projects, including book reviewing, music and theatre criticism, travel essays, advising several university presses, and lecturing. His other books include *Shirley Ann Grau* (Twayne, 1981) and, with his wife, June Schlueter, three reference works, most recently *An Encyclopedia of British Women Writers* (Garland, 1988).

In the 1960s he wrote one of the first doctoral dissertations about Doris Lessing, subsequently published in revised form as the first scholarly book about Doris Lessing (*The Novels of Doris Lessing*, Southern Illinois University Press, 1973), as well as many essays, lectures, and other works on her. In 1971 he started the Doris Lessing Seminars at the annual meetings of the Modern Language Association that subsequently grew into the Doris Lessing Society and has served as editor of the society's publication, *The Doris Lessing Newsletter*.

Doris Lessing

Going Home

'Africa belongs to the Africans; the sooner they take it back the better. But – a country also belongs to those who feel at home in it. Perhaps it may be that love of Africa the country will be strong enough to link people who hate each other now. Perhaps . . .'

Journeying back to the Rhodesia – modern-day Zimbabwe – in which she grew up, Doris Lessing is at her most formidable in this powerful, evocative account of life in a world divided by 'white supremacy' rule. From touching personal encounters with old and new friends to inimitable political interviews which effortlessly debunk the prejudices of prime ministers and union leaders alike, *Going Home* is a book of hope, a testament to those who fight apartheid, a vivid portrait of the people – black and white – who have shaped and will shape a great country.

'Mrs Lessing has captured the sight and sound and smell of Africa, and put it down on paper so that it may become real and tangible to those who have never set foot on African soil. This perhaps is her greatest achievement.'   *Sunday Times*

'I do not know of any other book that more immediately conveys the pathetic quality of settler life; some of her sketches have more of the truth of settler life in a few pages than other writers have managed to convey in as many volumes.'   Basil Davidson, *Tribune*

 flamingo

Doris Lessing

The Golden Notebook

'*The Golden Notebook* is euphoric, exhilarating, full of promise and provocation.'   *Vogue*

Anna Wulf is a young novelist with writer's block. Divorced, with a young child, and disillusioned by unsatisfactory relationships, she feels her life is falling apart. In fear of madness, she records her experiences in four coloured notebooks. The black notebook addresses her problems as a writer; the red her political life; the yellow her relationships and emotions; and the blue becomes a diary of everyday events. But it is a fifth notebook – the Golden Notebook – which is the key to her recovery and renaissance.

Bold and illuminating, fusing sex, politics, madness and motherhood, *The Golden Notebook* is at once a bold and perceptive portrait of the intellectual and moral climate of the 1950s – a society on the brink of feminism – and a powerful and revealing account of a woman searching for her own personal and political identity.

'Doris Lessing is a pioneer of feminist self-consciousness in its raw state . . . The truths contained in *The Golden Notebook* are indeed harsh. It can also be said that these particular truths have not been examined in so rigorous and exemplary a fashion since the first appearance of this extraordinary book. A seminal work.'
Anita Brookner, *London Review of Books*

'*The Golden Notebook* is the diary of a writer in shock, a young woman determined to forge a life as a 'free woman', as an 'intellectual'. Doris Lessing is a writer of considerable power, someone who can close her eyes and 'give' a situation by the sheer force of her emotional energy.'   Joan Didion, *New York Times*

flamingo